Blackst⌐⌐⌐
and the
Scourge of Europe

Tall, dark, elegant and tough, Blackstone grew up in the roughest slums of London. He now rubs shoulders with high society as easily as he moves among the thieves, whores and cut-throats of the nineteenth-century underworld. His dangerous career has made him a crack shot – and given him a taste for good wine and fine women. He is ruthless and courageous, and above all a Bow Street Runner.

Blackstone and the Scourge of Europe is the fourth Blackstone novel.

Blackstone and the Scourge of Europe

Richard Falkirk

THISTLE
PUBLISHING

To Martin, my son,
who thought of the name Blackstone

Author's Note

Among the many books I consulted for this novel I am particularly indebted to Gilbert Martineau's *Napoleon's St Helena* and *St Helena During Napoleon's Exile – Gorrequer's Diary* presented by James Kemble.

I should also like to thank Mr Leslie Honeywill, an authority on the history of submarines, for his help over a few pints of ale in the Market House Inn, Newton Abbot, Devon – a tavern which Blackstone would have appreciated.

PART ONE

CHAPTER ONE

They made an incongruous couple. The huge Negro, his bate torso sheathed with a slave's muscles; the Chinaman half his size, his pigeon frame clothed in cotton. When a cloud covered the moon the Negro's body merged with the night and it seemed as if the Chinaman were casting a giant shadow.

They headed north from the Briars, skirting Alarm House and its warning cannon, avoiding the Seine Valley and the Devil's Punch Bowl where stunted trees and black rocks made it a haunted place after nightfall. The air smelled of eucalyptus and geraniums and the sea.

Now they could hear the waves whispering on the shores of the island fortress where every man, woman and child was a prisoner of a kind. At 3 a.m., having successfully dodged the guards and sentries scattered over the plains and precipitous cliffs, the couple arrived at Sandy Bay.

The Negro pointed out to sea where two British men-o'-war lay at anchor and said: "They should be here at any moment." The Negro's name was Hannibal and, twenty years ago, he had been bought for £5 on the West African coast 1,140 miles away.

The Chinaman, named Wong Fu – but known as Number Thirteen in a community where Chinese servants merited numbers and Negroes bizarre names such as Caesar or

Fortescue – shook his head. "Not for another five minutes." His voice was tinsel compared with the Negro's deep tones; but it was he who wielded the authority. "Is the chest safe?" he asked.

Hannibal moved a rock as though it were a pebble. "Yes, it's here." He opened the lid and the moonlight glinted on a battery of bottles.

"It's good wine," Number Thirteen remarked. "Too good for the English. Odd, isn't it, that we should be smuggling wine from the vanquished to the victors."

Sometimes Hannibal had difficulty in understanding the little yellow man who worked in the French library and he didn't reply. In any case he preferred raw cane spirit to wine.

Wine stolen from the cellars of the "Frogs" was common currency on an island where supplies of liquor to drink with salt beef or atrophied chicken frequently ran low. And the ability of the French to maintain a good cellar infuriated the Governor, Sir Hudson Lowe. "Typical," he asserted, adding good housekeeping to the various manifestations of Gallic decadence.

"I hope nothing can go wrong," Hannibal remarked after five minutes had passed.

"What can go wrong?" Number Thirteen asked. "The look-outs have been bribed. The admiral wants his wine and the British Navy will see that he gets it. After all, they rule the waves, don't they?"

"I suppose so."

"All we've got to do is wait for the cutter, hand over the wine, collect our money and go home."

"I suppose so." Hannibal, arms folded across his chest, stared across the quicksilver sea in what he thought might be the direction of England; once a slave set foot on English soil he was free and every piastre Hannibal earned from petty crime was saved for his passage to freedom; certain reforms regarding slaves were supposed to have taken place on the island, but Hannibal had noticed little change – he still lived in a cell with a stone for a pillow, he had been flogged for stealing three sweet potatoes and his brother had recently been sold for £50.

Hannibal said: "They're late."

"A few minutes doesn't matter," Number Thirteen said.

"We should have seen them by now."

"Not necessarily. They're coming along the shore. They've been on patrol." Number Thirteen gestured to his right towards Potato Bay and Lot's Wife's Beach. "Perhaps there's been an incident. Another scare."

"Or perhaps…." The Negro began to shiver.

"Perhaps what?"

"Nothing." Hannibal hugged his chest, trying to control the trembling. He noticed a movement on the sea between the shore and the two British ships and a violent spasm of shivering shook his frame. He pointed without speaking.

The Chinaman shaded his eyes although it was night. "What? I can't see anything."

"There." Hannibal moaned. The sweaty night air froze on his body.

Number Thirteen laughed; a worried laugh. "A shark fin," he told Hannibal. "They've been dumping rotten meat off the ships." But he knew the British Navy devoured its rotten meat down to the last maggot.

Hannibal said: "I'm going."

"Don't be a fool. It's taken a month to get this wine."

A cloud slid across the moon, the darkness erasing the movement on the sea. They listened to the waves, to the chirp of crickets, the breeze in the thickets; only the stars were silent.

"You see," Number Thirteen said, trying to swallow the quaver in his voice. "It was the light on the waves. An optical illusion," he assured himself.

"Holy Mother of God," said Hannibal, sinking to his knees and pointing at the stars. Number Thirteen looked up in time to see a shooting star fade in the sky. It wasn't a night for superstitious slaves. "Sweet Jesus," said Hannibal, "forgive me. ..." He looked up at the Chinaman. "It means a death."

The clouds slipped past the moon and the ocean was silvered once more, the two brigantines with their oil lamps and candle-lanterns looking like glowworms.

Hannibal was paralysed on his knees and the little Chinaman had discovered that erudition wasn't helping him with the phenomena of this October night in 1820. The Negro babbled to God and to the Chinaman at his side – until he realised that Number Thirteen was no longer there. He jumped to his feet; fifty yards behind him he made out the figure of the imperturbable, enigmatic Chinaman running like hell.

Hannibal took to his heels in pursuit, catching up with Number Thirteen somewhere on the farmland owned by Sir William Doveton. They didn't speak: there was nothing to say.

Soon afterwards Hannibal struck left towards Plantation House, the home of the Governor of St Helena. The Chinaman struck right on his longer journey towards Longwood House, the residence of Napoleon Bonaparte, for whom he worked.

Chapter Two

The King is dead! Long live the King!

A mad monarch had died and a buffoon had taken his place. And Edmund Blackstone, Bow Street Runner, was, to his chagrin, guarding George Augustus Frederick, Prince of Wales, Prince Regent and now, at the age of fifty-nine, George IV – although, as yet, uncrowned.

Prinny, as the people still called him, was giving a banquet at the Royal Pavilion, Brighton, his Xanadu. Half an hour before the guests were due, Blackstone prowled the extravagant chambers looking for any threat of danger to the King. That part of him trained to maintain law and order approved his vigilance; that part which never forgot his childhood in a stinking London rookery applauded the intentions of anyone to assassinate the plump sybarite on the throne of England.

Blackstone walked from the Octagon Hall, through the vestibule to the corridor where George's dream of the orient enfolded him: model junks, waterlily chandelier hung from a dragon, simulated bamboo made from cast-iron, Chinese banners, Chinese lanterns, Chinese figures lurking in the recesses in the pink walls leafed with sky-blue foliage. It was summer and the heat from the patent stoves and the new gas lighting made the atmosphere stifling.

From the corridor Blackstone made his way to the banqueting room to which John Nash had just put the finishing touches. From the domed ceiling a silver dragon held a thirty-foot-long gasolier, weighing a ton, made from pearls and rubies. It had cost £5,613 19s. Enough to rebuild the Holborn Rookery? One faulty fitting and it could crush the pear-shaped monarch.

Blackstone inspected more Chinese splendours: dragons writhing everywhere, lacquer doors, crimson draperies and golden murals of Cathay, one showing a lady said to be a likeness of Lady Conyngham, one of George's mistresses.

He ran his hand over a tall lamp made from blue Spode porcelain, wood and ormolu, by Robert Jones. Again the division of feeling. Blackstone, student of *objets d'art* with an embryonic collection in his rooms in Paddington Village, admired the King's taste which had given England so much beauty, so many fine buildings, but rejected the lack of feeling which bankrupted honest men to give substance to his aesthetic dreams.

Blackstone shook his head, checked the Manton pocket pistol in the trouser pocket of his evening clothes and headed for regions where he was more at home. The kitchens.

But they were like no kitchens he had ever seen before. No crusty frying pans with sausages becalmed in black fat, no smuts suspended in the air, no babies starving on the floor while their mothers supped sixpenny-worth of gin. This kitchen was supported by cast-iron pillars surmounted by copper palm fronds, the walls were lined with 550 gleaming copper pots and pans; the fireplace was hooded with a bronze canopy; the tables were hidden with a gluttony of food.

Some forty cooks laboured under the directions of the French chef, successor to Carême, the inventor of caramel. It was reputed that the new chef could only produce his finest work after he had fondled the breasts of a couple of kitchen maids. Today's menu consisted of ninety-four dishes and, when Blackstone arrived, the chef was feeling the breasts of a plump pantry maid.

He took a ladle and sampled some soup. But, with ninety-four dishes, a poisoner would have to have intimate knowledge of the Royal palate, otherwise he would become a mass murderer.

The flushed pantry maid, buttoning up her white blouse after the attentions of the chef, said: "To your liking, *sir?*"

Blackstone appraised the vanishing bosom. "Delicious," he said.

"I meant the soup."

"That's good, too."

"And who may you be, *sir?*" No servility there; she recognises her own kind, Blackstone thought.

"My name's Blackstone."

"The Bow Street Runner?"

Blackstone admitted it.

"I once went to Bow Street. The master I was working for accused me of filching a silver salt-cellar. But I threatened to tell her ladyship about his visits to my room and he dropped the charge."

"Could you prove it?" asked Blackstone.

"He had a birthmark," the girl said.

"Ah," Blackstone murmured. "And did you filch the salt cellar?"

"None of your business, you being a thief-taker."

Blackstone grinned. "You're the sort of thief one enjoys taking."

"None of your cheek," she said in a pleased voice, adding: "You could be a thief yourself. You don't look as if you're on the side of the law. But," she said wisely, "I suppose that's all to the good in your job."

Blackstone shrugged; she was right, his appearance was his strength and he wasn't proud of it. Luck and a benefactor had lifted him from the underworld of London's stews and deposited him on the right side of the law. With his gilt-crowned baton he now protected the rules he had once joyously broken; but he preserved his own interpretation of evil. He never noticed a bare-footed urchin with a sharp, starved face smatter-hauling a gentleman's silk handkerchief: he never failed to notice – and arrest – a sweep stuffing an urchin with bleeding elbows and knees up a chimney.

"Don't look so solemn," the girl said. "I didn't mean it about you being a thief. Honest."

"Well you were right," Blackstone told her. "I was a thief."

"Strike me blind," exclaimed the girl. "And a prize-fighter by the looks of you."

"I've done a bit of milling," Blackstone admitted. He pointed at the steaming tureens which the *chefs de cuisine* were taking to the Decker's Room for collection by scarlet-liveried footmen. "Do you know if there's any particular dish for Prinny?"

"Don't ask me, ask the Frog," nodding at the French chef. "But I bet that's his favourite soup."

Blackstone followed her gaze to a silver bowl of bubbling liquid into which a male cook was spitting.

"Here," exclaimed the girl, "I'd best be getting on or the Frog will throw me out. Sort of tit-for-tat," she grinned. Her expression was momentarily wistful. "I suppose you'll be off after the guests have finished stuffing themselves?"

Blackstone thought about it. When George, the First Gentleman of Europe, departed for Windsor, he would have to go with him. But the First Gentleman would probably be so drunk that he would sleep the night in Brighton. No, he told the girl, he wasn't in a hurry to be off.

"You'll be staying here, I suppose?"

"Do you know of a better place?"

"I might."

"Then I'll buy you a tankard of ale when our work is finished."

She winked and scuttered away as the French chef approached, hands fondling invisible bosoms. Blackstone left as well: the chef only spoke French and Blackstone only spoke English.

The vast dining table beneath the gasolier was a battlefield. Soups, sucking pigs, larks, patés, fish and fowl, water ices, fruit and cheese had been assaulted, mauled and dumped. Spilled wine was the blood among the carnage.

George, flanked by Lady Conyngham and a French envoy from Paris, presided, sweat trickling down his powdered cheeks. To the envoy he spoke fluent French, to Lady Conyngham he spoke amorously; every now and again he belched.

Watching from the wings, Blackstone hoped the King would drink enough to dispatch him into stupefied sleep for the night.

The French envoy was talking about Napoleon. "They say," he complained, "that he is being treated shamefully by your representative on St Helena, Sir Hudson Lowe. They say that this man Lowe is hated and that the Emperor is venerated. They say that in truth it is really the Emperor who rules the little rock as if it were his empire."

The King drank some wine. "Emperor?" he asked. "Did I hear you say Emperor?" He held his glass tightly in his dimpled fist.

The envoy, a sleek nobleman with black curls combed forward, said: "To the French, Napoleon Bonaparte is still Emperor." The wine was making his tongue brave.

"Ah, to the French. I sometimes wonder," the King said to those around him, "who won the war. To the French, indeed! The Gallic memory is short. Have you forgotten Wellington? Have you forgotten Waterloo? *General* Bonaparte, my friend, is a prisoner-of-war, nothing more. The Scourge of Europe is a tame, captive animal." He laughed and those around him laughed.

The Frenchman said: "Or a sleeping lion, perhaps."

"Or a toothless tiger," the King said.

"Cutting his second set of teeth," the Frenchman said.

"'Pon my soul," remarked the King, "you have the devil's own cheek."

"With respect, sire, the war has been over for more than five years. There is little point in prolonging enmity. I am merely repeating the gossip related by 'ships' captains and unofficial couriers who have visited St Helena. They say that Sir Hudson Lowe, a miserable fellow by all accounts, is jealous of his prisoner and is trying to break his spirit."

"And how should we treat the Corsican? Give him a throne? A grace-and-favour house in St James's? A duchy, perhaps?"

Lady Conyngham patted the King's hand which was resting on her thigh. "They do say there is a lot of support for Bonaparte in England, my love. Lord Holland and the Liberals, even Byron.... They all say that Bonaparte should be allowed to retain at least his dignity."

The King withdrew his hand. "Perhaps," he said, "they should reserve their noble sentiments for the preservation of the dignity of their own monarchy."

The Frenchman smiled. The smile seemed to imply: That is up to you, Your Majesty.

After the port and brandy the guests adjourned to the music room with its dome-and-tent ceiling, two pagodas, bamboo canopy above the organ and Chinese chandeliers. A forty-strong orchestra played light music and the King, his voice slightly slurred, sang "Lord Mornington's Waterfall" and "Life's a Bumper".

Blackstone sat beside a captain in the 45th Foot, Grenadier Company, and his wife. The wife was a vivacious girl with a mass of black ringlets, the slightest of casts in her eyes, and a mole in the crevice of her bosom. He yawned.

The captain's wife tapped him with her fan and whispered: "You're not a musical man, Mr Blackstone?"

"I prefer music-houses," Blackstone said.

"Ah, the music-houses." Her voice was wistful. "We don't frequent such places, more's the pity." She paused. "They say the King sings by ear."

"I don't doubt it," Blackstone said. "It's the sort of noise I should imagine an ear would make."

"You are very disrespectful, Mr Blackstone."

Blackstone regarded the rise and fall of the mole above her low-cut gown. "How do you know my name?"

"Weren't you the Bow Street Runner who distinguished himself at that dreadful Cato Street affair?"

"No," Blackstone told her. "That was Ruthven. I was the one who let one of the conspirators get away. A man called Challoner."

"I heard you were very brave." Blackstone wasn't sure whether there was admiration or mockery in her voice. "And you *have* distinguished yourself since."

"The trouble is," Blackstone said, "that the real villains are above the law." He gestured around the music room, yawned again, and took a pinch of Fribourg and Treyer snuff from his gold Nathaniel Mills snuffbox.

The guests were applauding the King's last song; for a moment Blackstone feared that he might give an encore. But he stumbled and made his way unsteadily to an armchair with legs fashioned like winged sphinxes.

The captain said: "That was delightful, wholly delightful."

His wife said: "Mr Blackstone doesn't seem to think so."

The captain peered at Blackstone. "Doesn't he, indeed." He frowned. "I don't think we've had the pleasure...."

His wife introduced them. The captain's name was Randolph Perkins and her name was Louise.

"One of the Runners, eh? I've heard all about your escapades," Perkins said, consigning Blackstone to the ranks of foot soldiers. "What the devil are you doing here?"

"Protecting the King," Blackstone said. "Making sure he doesn't strangle himself with his vocal chords."

"You are most disrespectful, sir!" Perkins was a slender, handsome man, fond of jewellery, with a reputation as a duellist; Blackstone could picture him carrying a bullet-torn flag in a beleaguered garrison.

"On the contrary," Blackstone said. "I do have respect for Prinny. He has fine taste and is making London into a beautiful city once more. He is courteous, amusing, generous and intelligent. He has one fault: he is King."

"Very well put, Mr Blackstone," Louise Perkins said. Her voice was low, barely hiding her amusement at the world. "I think Prinny's rather sweet," she said, "and rather sad. As you say, Mr Blackstone, he shouldn't be a king. He seeks flattery to reassure himself of his stature. If he weren't a monarch vanity wouldn't be necessary."

Her husband said: "My dear, you shouldn't talk about the King in that way. After all, it isn't the man we should consider" – he tightened his jaw muscles at the concession – "it's the monarchy itself. After all, I hold his commission."

His wife regarded him with her violet eyes. "Really? And a fat lot of good it's done us," she said. She had difficulty, Blackstone noticed, pronouncing her R's.

The orchestra launched itself into the national anthem. The guests lining the walls beneath azure drapes and lotus chandeliers stood respectfully; the men in red, green, yellow and blue military uniforms and black and white evening dress, the women in lace and silk falling tent-like from bust to floor.

Standing beside Louise Perkins, snuffbox in his hand, Blackstone felt her warmth as she brushed against him.

After the anthem one of the King's secretaries moved busily among the guests. There was, he whispered loudly, to be a nightcap for a dozen or so selected guests in the King's apartments; it was in no way a reflection on the majority – although the secretary's tone implied the opposite – but the subject to be discussed was private.

Louise Perkins said to Blackstone: "What a bore. I'm afraid we're invited." She smiled. "But you will be there as the guardian of our monarchy?"

"I'm afraid so," Blackstone said, wondering how long the pantry maid would wait.

"You know, of course, the subject of this *tête-à-tête?*"

"I've no idea," Blackstone said. "I'm only in attendance in case someone wants to drop a gasolier on His Majesty's head. We got this stupid job when a mad woman called Margaret Nicholson attacked George III in 1786. We get £200 a year for our trouble," he added.

Randolph Perkins offered his wife his arm. "In fact," he said to Blackstone, "the reason for this extra hospitality is Napoleon Bonaparte. There is reason to believe that an escape is being planned. But, of course, as a Bow Street Runner you would know all about that."

"On the contrary," Blackstone told him, "we have nothing whatsoever to do with arranging poor old Boney's escape." He fingered his Manton, wondering if a duel with Perkins would lighten the boredom of royal duties.

Louise Perkins said: "The truth of the matter is that Randolph has been posted to St Helena as a special emissary to report on the security situation there."

"Please," Perkins said abruptly, "you forget yourself, Louise."

"Do I? I seem to be very much aware of myself at this moment."

Blackstone said: "Don't worry, culley...."

"I think you forget my rank," Perkins interrupted. He stroked his blonde moustache as if it were a badge of authority.

Blackstone yawned again. "Why should I forget your rank?" he asked, slipping the snuffbox back into his pocket. "It was bought for you, wasn't it? I never forget anything that's bought for a good price."

Perkins began: "Now look here...."

Blackstone fished out his baton with the gilt crown. "And you look here, my covey, you are responsible for your wife's debts."

"What's that got to do with anything?"

"You could compare indiscretions with debts."

"I don't see...."

"Your wife has just informed me that you are to be posted to St Helena to investigate the security situation on the island where Napoleon Bonaparte is held prisoner. Isn't that correct?" Before Perkins could answer, Blackstone went on: "As far as I am concerned that is a breach of security. It could well be my duty to inform His Majesty that an officer whose wife is capable of such indiscretions is not a fit man to be entrusted with such a delicate post."

They gathered in the library with its candelabra, furniture by Thomas Hope and George Smith, and lime-green walls and ceiling. In an ante-room into which the impertinent glanced stood the King's sea-water bath.

The fifty-nine-year-old King's eyes were clouded and Blackstone wondered if he had taken laudanum between dinner and night-cap.

Robert Peel, the former Chief Secretary for Ireland who had formed the Irish Constabulary, the Peelers, was present. Blackstone knew that he was in the company of an enemy. If Peel – tipped to be the next Home Secretary – had his way, the Bow Street Runners were finished.

Champagne circulated while the ladies fanned themselves and the men talked about Napoleon.

The King said to Peel: "What about these rumours of an escape in the offing?" He sat squashed into a lacquer chair.

Peel, austere, honourable and – Blackstone thought – as cold-blooded as a snake, said: "It is not a matter for me, Your Majesty. Although, like everyone in London, I have heard rumours that Bonaparte is planning to leave St Helena just as he left Elba."

The King pawed at the sweat trickling down his cheeks. "Stuff and nonsense. Bonaparte is a sick man. He's middle-aged and fat and suffering from some stomach ailment," said the King, as if he himself were lithe and fit.

Peel shrugged. "They are only rumours. As you know, it has also been rumoured that Bonaparte has already flown."

"And that *is* nonsense." The King waved his hand, finding the comforting fingers of Lady Conyngham. "If Bonaparte had left St Helena then we'd know about it. Damn it, man, he would have joined brother Joseph in America and the whole world would have known."

"I agree, Your Majesty," Peel said. "I am inclined to believe that Bonaparte is still on St Helena. And he *is* a very sick man. I doubt if even he is in a fit state to contemplate escape."

The King looked around him and noticed Captain Perkins. "Who's that?" he asked.

The secretary whispered in the King's ear. The King nodded and beckoned Perkins and his wife. "Ah, so you're the young man who's going to make sure that General Bonaparte is in safe hands."

Perkins bowed low. "I shall do my best, Your Majesty."

The King slopped some champagne on the red sash across his chest. "Do you have any notion of what security measures there should be in force to discourage Bonaparte from escaping?"

"I have experience of military security, Your Majesty."

"Have you," the King murmured. "Have you indeed." He gestured with his glass, dismissing Perkins, and turned to Peel. "What are the grounds for supposing there is a security risk?"

Peel shrugged. "It is not my responsibility, Your Majesty...."

"It may not be your responsibility," the King interrupted him. "But you have your ear close to the ground. What are the rumours?"

Peel said: "As Your Majesty knows, messages in cypher appeared in the weekly journal *The Anti-Gallican* three years ago. Despite its title there was reason to suppose that it was being used as a medium to transmit messages between Bonaparte and his supporters. The editor, Lewis Goldsmith, was known to have been a double agent, a blackmailer, and was once paid two million francs to undertake a mission to

Germany for the Emperor – the then Emperor," Peel corrected himself.

The King winced as gout throbbed in his foot. "That was three years ago. According to recent reports from St Helena, Napoleon would have to escape in a bath-chair."

"There have been other messages, Your Majesty, in other journals. They would appear to emanate from the Champ d'Asile, the followers of Napoleon who want him to rule over them in America. His brother Joseph has settled in Philadelphia where, as Grand Master of the Grand Orient of France, he has a great deal of masonic support."

The King said: "Napoleon loose among the Americans! That would teach them, eh?" He spoke to the secretary and two footmen put a stool under his foot. His eyelids were beginning to droop, his foot twitched with a life of its own. "How seriously do you take all this, sir?"

Peel said: "The question, Your Majesty, should be addressed to Lord Bathurst."

"But he's not here and I'm addressing it to you."

Peel shrugged. "With a man like Bonaparte you can never be too careful."

Lounging beside the bookshelves in the corner of the room, Blackstone glanced at an Egyptian clock. Nearly midnight. The pantry maid would be waiting, contemplating, perhaps, a visit to the French chef's chambers if he didn't turn up. He wished to God the King would pass out.

Louise Perkins wandered over to him. "You're scowling with boredom," she told him. "Do you have another … appointment?"

"I have to question a member of the staff," Blackstone said.

"Poor old Prinny," Louise Perkins said. "You know what's happening, of course. He's at last become King and all he's heard all night is the esteem in which the British public hold Napoleon. He's madly jealous, poor soul, and drunk at the same time."

"He's certainly kanurd," Blackstone said.

"Kanurd, Mr Blackstone?"

"Drunk," Blackstone said. "Lushy."

"It must be exciting mixing with the dangerous classes." Her violet eyes seemed to look beyond him.

"More exciting than mixing with the effete classes."

The secretary bustled up. "Mr Blackstone, the King wishes words with you."

The King stared at Blackstone through pink eyes closing into slits in the cushions of his face. "Ah," he said, "the redoubtable Bow Street Runner. Redoubtable in many ways, eh, Mr Blackstone?"

"Your Majesty?"

"The ladies of the household have been speaking most favourably of you, Mr Blackstone. Even my Lady Conyngham here. Isn't that right, my dear?"

Lady Conyngham smiled over her fan at Blackstone.

Blackstone thought that most of the King's mistresses would look well in his collection of antiques.

The King said: "Do you enjoy your duties as my guardian, Mr Blackstone?"

"I am honoured to serve you, Your Majesty." Blackstone put his hand to his mouth; the yawns were surfacing like champagne bubbles.

"Bored, Mr Blackstone?"

"On the contrary, Your Majesty."

"Life at Court must be very boring for one so active – and virile – as yourself." The King turned to Peel. "You have decided views about the Runners, I believe?"

"I have decided views about how a proper police force should be run, Your Majesty."

"The Runners have a fine record for catching criminals."

"So did the old thief-takers."

"Set a thief to catch a thief, eh?"

"Their methods of recovering stolen property are, to say the least, questionable, Your Majesty. It does not seem to me to be in the interests of justice to do a deal with a thief in which the victim recovers his property after the thief *and* the Bow Street Runner have taken a percentage."

Blackstone said: "However, you will agree, sir, that the Runners are efficient in preventing murders masquerading as duels."

Peel, who in 1815 had gone to Ostend to duel with the Irishman O'Connell, flushed.

The King said: "I can vouchsafe that Mr Blackstone is an excellent guardian. I am still alive – just. I decided yesterday that Mr Blackstone should be entrusted with more important duties than protecting a monarch who so evidently bores him. Also I feel that the ladies should be protected from such an excessively virile presence." He hoisted his body up in the chair and smiled at Blackstone. "I think, sir, that you should be entrusted with the security of a man who, in some quarters, is held in more esteem than their own monarch. I am not altogether satisfied that Captain Perkins is experienced enough in the sort of villainy that he will encounter. He will investigate security from the military point of view. You, sir, will employ your undoubted talents gleaned from your underworld contacts to make your own assessment of the possibilities of escape."

Blackstone's yawns were strangled. "I don't quite understand, Your Majesty."

"It's very simple," the King said. "You will sail with Captain Perkins to St Helena on the next boat. You will have ample time to compare the boredom of the Court of St James's with the atmosphere of General Bonaparte's rock." The King closed his eyes and, after a few moments, began to snore.

The pantry maid was cross. "You're late," she said.

Blackstone said: "I need a drink."

They went to a tavern frequented by the staff of the Royal Pavilion and members of the underworld who came down from London to rob and swindle the swells and dandies who had decided that sea-water was the cure for dissipation.

The atmosphere changed as Blackstone went in: it always did. He ordered two dog's noses, watching impatiently as the serving girl mixed the warm porter, moist sugar, gin and nutmeg.

"You're not in a very good mood," the pantry maid observed.

"Would you be if you had just been sent to gaol?" He watched a mutcher who specialised in stealing from drunks make a hasty exit from the tavern.

He turned to a pickpocket hastily drinking up his ale at the next table. "Good evening, Harry," he said. "What's happened to the look-out system? No crows outside watching for the law?"

"We didn't expect a Runner here," the pickpocket said. "Who are you after?" He whispered furtively. "Can I be of any help, Mr Blackstone?"

"You can," Blackstone said, sipping his drink. "When you go back to the Rookery tell them they can relax – I'm going away. Tell them Edmund Blackstone has been deported."

The pickpocket looked pleased. "Straight up, Mr Blackstone?"

"Don't look so happy about it," Blackstone said. He leaned across and lifted a gold watch from the sack-like inside pocket of the pickpocket's jacket. "Still tooling, eh, Harry? Who did you lift that from?"

"It's mine," the pickpocket said unhappily.

Blackstone examined it and asked: "Since when was your name Randolph Perkins?"

"A gentleman of that name sold it to me."

"And I'm buying it from you for the same price you paid for it," Blackstone said, pocketing the watch. "Now off to Holborn with you, Harry, and spread the good word."

The pickpocket scuttled out of the tavern.

Blackstone ordered two more dog's noses.

"What's all this about being deported?" the girl asked.

"I'm going to St Helena on my holidays. Want to come?"

"Is it near Brighton?"

"It's near nowhere," he told her. He finished his drink. "Come on," he said, "I'll see you home. The protection of young ladies abroad at night is part of my duties."

Later, in her room, she asked: "Was that part of your duties as well?"

He grinned. "The last wish of a condemned man," he said.

CHAPTER THREE

From the deck of the brig, St Helena looked like a fortress; steep cliffs plunging into the sea, the settlement of Jamestown like the nest of some predatory bird built in a cleft.

Sea, sky and island were grey. Waves ringed the coast with spray, a few gulls hung in the misty air which fused sea and sky on the horizon.

Blackstone, who had been taking French lessons from Louise Perkins and reading up the history of Napoleon's exile, recalled the first reaction of the fallen emperor whose empire had been shrunk to this crag in the Atlantic. "It is not an attractive place," he had said. "I should have done better to remain in Egypt."

One of the ladies in his party had put it more succinctly. "The devil must have shit the island as it flew from one world to the other," she had observed.

Perkins said: "Nowhere looks attractive from the approaches. They say the houses on the plateau have a most pleasing appearance."

The brig sailed round the southern shore of the island and entered Jamestown harbour from the west. Blackstone and the Perkins gazed at a huddle of houses, a jetty, a church, three palm trees and, spiking the encircling mountains, the cannons installed to stop one man escaping.

A small crowd had gathered on the quayside. Blackstone guessed that the arrival of a ship from Britain was the high point of their existence.

Louise Perkins shivered and her husband put his arm round her. "It will be different in the summer, my dear," he said.

Blackstone said: "This *is* their summer."

Perkins said: "I shall want to see you tomorrow morning, after I've met the Governor, to discuss tactics."

"Will you now," Blackstone said.

"Come to our lodgings at eleven." Perkins handed Blackstone a piece of paper with an address on it. "After I've outlined my plans we'll make a tour of the island."

"I'll look forward to that," Blackstone said.

They boarded the cutter and entered the fortress walls.

Blackstone had been on the island just two hours when the first attempt was made on his life. It made him feel more at home.

An official of the East India Company had found him lodgings in a tavern in Jamestown frequented by soldiers and sailors and he had laid out his clothes and checked his guns. He had with him his favourite Mantons, one of the new Collier revolvers with a tapered barrel and a self-priming cover, a set of duelling pistols by Durs Egg, a vicious spring-bayonet musket made in Bayonne and a blunderbuss from a Royal Mail that would blow a man's head off at short range and be as effective as hailstones at a longer distance. He also had with him a French stiletto inside his boot next to his calf.

The rum toddy a maid had brought him stood untouched on the table; Blackstone didn't like rum.

He had washed and shaved and dressed with care in white breeches, soft Hoby boots that never wore out, blue swallow-tail coat and white shirt. He sat on the side of the bed, took a pinch of snuff and listened to sounds of revelry from the parlour at the end of the passage; perhaps St Helena wasn't as bad as it looked; in any case the Neighbour, as they called Napoleon here, wouldn't last another twelve months.

He decided to rest for a while and, taking off his coat, lay back on the bed, hands behind his head, thinking about Louise Perkins and the advances she had made on board ship; he hadn't responded because other men's wives were not his style, although her approaches had become more seductive as the voyage progressed, particularly, he suspected, in French, a language which was proving elusive to him. He wondered if those slightly crossed eyes of hers straightened out when she made love.

It was dark when his instincts told him there was someone outside the door. With one hand he cocked the Manton pocket pistol on the chest of drawers beside the bed, with the other he eased the stiletto half out of his boot.

The key turned quietly as if the lock had recently been oiled. He heard someone breathing unevenly as they concentrated on stealth. Blackstone caressed the butt of the pistol. A floorboard creaked; all movement stopped as the intruder froze. Then the sound of a breath being exhaled. Blackstone thought he could see the outline of a man in the darkness but he wasn't sure because the only light was from the stars. He considered shooting from the chest of drawers, but if he missed, the intruder would be on him as he struggled to rise from the bed.

He waited.

The figure approached, a vague outline thickening. But there was something wrong; even in the darkness the shape was too indistinct.

The arm was descending before Blackstone realised what was happening. He heaved himself to one side as a knife cut through the sleeve of his shirt, puncturing the mattress. Blackstone drew back one foot and kicked at the vague figure beside the bed. A grunt of pain. Blackstone's sleeve was freed as the man raised the knife again. Blackstone rolled on to the floor as the knife plunged down, ripping the pillow.

Blackstone crouched on the floor. He could just make out a pair of eyes gleaming. He drew the stiletto. The man was edging round the bed, grunting as his shin caught the metal. Blackstone was acutely aware of the starlight shining on his own white shirtfront. He knew that the man was very big; he knew that he had left the Manton on the far side of the bed when he rolled clear.

As the intruder came round the bed, Blackstone vaulted across it so that the bed was between them. He groped for the pistol and heard it clatter to the ground. He heaved the bed and his assailant fell against the wall. Blackstone followed through, stiletto in hand, butting with his head.

The metallic sound of a knife hitting the floor. Two powerful hands gripping his forearms. His grip on the stiletto weakening. He could smell the man's sweat. He brought his knee up into his crotch; the man retched, the grip loosened on Blackstone's arms.

At that moment Blackstone realised that he had an advantage. His assailant was incredibly strong but he wasn't an ally-cat fighter. He doesn't know the tricks, Blackstone thought, butting again at the flash of teeth in front of him. But, as he bent forward retching, the assailant had managed to pick up the knife. Blackstone saw it glint like a silver fish in the starlight and ducked as it slashed past his face.

Blackstone hooked at the attacker's knees with one leg; the man crashed against the wall, dropping the knife again. Blackstone went in with the stiletto, feeling it cut flesh. The man gave a strange, gurgling scream; there was a warm wetness on the handle of the stiletto.

"Right, culley," Blackstone whispered. "One more move and this cuts your throat."

The man twisted away and Blackstone felt the tearing of flesh. He dived after him but his foot slipped on blood. Blackstone poised himself: when the escaping man opened the door he would throw the stiletto. They both paused, breath rasping.

The shattering of wood and splintering of broken glass took Blackstone by surprise. For a fraction of a second his reactions seized up. When he reached the wrecked window he could see the man crouching in the shadows outside.

Blackstone leapt through the window as his attacker ran down the street into the night. He saw him once more, hesitating at the end of a side-street; then he was gone and Blackstone was alone listening to the chirp of the crickets and the sound of the waves.

The tavern was nicknamed the Good Neighbour, a name which had infuriated the Governor, who was unduly sensitive to any sympathy towards Napoleon. It was run by a one-armed landlord called Jack Darnell and his daughter Lucinda. Both had been smugglers in Devon, associates of the notorious freetrader John Rattenbury.

Lucinda wasn't pleased to see her guest.

"God blind me," she said when Blackstone walked into the parlour. "I knew we had a new guest but I didn't dream it was you. What brings you of all people to this God-forsaken place?"

Blackstone, who was equally surprised to see Lucinda Darnell, said: "I always thought you'd end your days in Exeter Gaol."

He sat at her table and ordered a brandy. The parlour was packed with soldiers and sailors, many of them drunk, and in one comer three French servants from Longwood House were deep in conversation with Jack Darnell.

Blackstone sipped his brandy apprehensively. "A nice drop," he said. "Contraband, I presume?"

Lucinda, wild and red-haired and wearing gypsy earrings, glared at him. "Surely Edmund Blackstone hasn't come all this way looking for smugglers. I should have thought," she said, "that you would have purged yourself of freetraders by now."

Blackstone had once been dispatched to Devon to trap the crooked magistrates collaborating with the smugglers. He'd stayed at the Mount Pleasant Inn at Dawlish Warren where contraband was stored in secret caverns. He had been employed by Darnell as a flasherman to communicate with cutters loaded with liquor from Cherbourg, Roscoff and the Channel Isles waiting in the mouth of the Exe. He became quite expert with the long-funnelled lanterns which the more sophisticated flashermen used.

As always, his loyalties were divided: he was happy to bring the corrupt justices to their own justice, but loathe to penalise the swashbuckling privateers who were hero-worshipped by the people. The magistrates were bribed with Cognac, wine, Hollands and Crow Link schnapps and the spoils were divided in the catacombs of a "haunted" church – the ghosts being friendly to smugglers and hostile to revenue men.

With two other Runners he planned to ambush the magistrates as they rode home with their liquor. But the plan misfired when the smugglers came to the rescue; there was a skirmish and Jack Darnell's arm was blown off.

"Yes," said Lucinda, pointing at her father's back, "I should have thought you would have been satisfied shooting an honest man's arm off."

"An *honest* man's arm?" Blackstone shook his head. "I didn't do that, Lucy, and you know it. You also know that I did everything in my power to help the lot of you get away."

"You betrayed us," she said.

"I put three corrupt rogues hiding behind the law behind bars."

"Are they the only ones hiding behind the law, Blackie?" Her tone had softened: she had once been very fond of the rugged flasherman and had visited him at his lonely post overlooking the salt marshes where the kegs of liquor were transported to the Mount Pleasant Inn.

Blackstone tossed back his brandy and ordered another tot for each of them. "You know where to hit me, don't you. You always did," he added reflectively.

"I know you're not proud of what you do."

"You're wrong," Blackstone said. "But sometimes I have difficulty in accepting that because something's legal it's good."

"A lawman posing as a smuggler...that must have tested you."

"It did," Blackstone said.

"What are you here for, Blackie?"

"A truce," Blackstone told her. "I think that's the first priority."

"You didn't know I was here?"

Blackstone shook his head. "Neither you nor your father. Which brings me to the question, What are you doing here?"

Lucinda Darnell looked confused. "It's a long story...."

"Tell it then."

"I'll cut it short. I got engaged to an official of the East India Company who virtually own this rock – at least they did until the Neighbour arrived. This fellow was posted here and he said he could arrange for my father to take over this tavern. So here we are, Blackie. At least I tried to become an honest woman."

Blackstone took some snuff, reflecting that a marriage between the Queen of the Smugglers and a trading official was an unlikely match. "Where is the lucky man?" he asked.

"Ah, thereby hangs another tale."

"He didn't disappear mysteriously like that revenue man whose body was found lying in a pool at Dawlish Warren."

They stopped talking to watch a soldier in scarlet and a sailor brawling over the favours of a Negress. When the sailor drew a knife, two of Darnell's henchmen moved in, disarmed the sailor and tossed both of them into the street. The Negress began to bargain with one of the Frenchmen who had gone up to the bar.

Lucinda ordered more brandy; she had always had a masculine capacity for liquor, Blackstone recalled.

She said: "No, he didn't disappear quite like that. Sir Hudson Lowe decided that he was spying for the French and had him thrown off the island."

"And you, of course, will follow him?"

She laughed and the gold ear-rings shaped like tiny casks jingled. "I like this tavern. It was part of the bargain. I can't help it if he was stupid enough to get caught. Although I think he was as innocent as a new-born babe. Sir Hudson, or the Lackey as he's known here, is touched up here" – she tapped her forehead – "on the subject of Boney."

An object crashed on to the table between them. A wooden arm with a hook on the end of it. On the other end was Jack Darnell, a huge man with a beard and a face leathered by salt water spraying over the bows of a smuggler's cutter.

"What in damnation are you doing here?" Darnell said. "The one man I prayed I would never set eyes on again. Edmund Blackstone! May your soul rot in hell." Blackstone thought the anger had a theatrical ring to it.

"Sit down, Jack," Blackstone said. "We must have words."

"Sit down with a lawman who blew off my arm? No, culley, the only seat I'd take with you would be your coffin."

"Imagine that chair's my coffin," Blackstone said, calling for more brandy.

The old smuggler sat down and Blackstone repeated his defence. "If they'd sent another Runner instead of me you'd be rotting in Exeter Gaol now instead of making a deal with the French to buy lush pinched from Napoleon's cellars."

"As tricky as ever, eh, Blackie? Is that what you're here for, to persecute old Jack Darnell?" He waved his hooked arm at Blackstone. "You know as well as I do that it's no offence to sell contraband, only to smuggle it."

"Aye," Blackstone agreed. "But this happens to be stolen liquor if I'm not much mistaken." He kept one hand on his pocket pistol. "But that's not what I'm here for, Jack. I want a truce and I want your help. You'll have the ear of the French, no doubt, and every tavern is the sorting house of gossip. Keep your ear to the grog, Jack, and you, Lucy, and let me know what you hear about plans for Boney's escape."

"The whole island's seething with rumours," Lucy told him. "But it always has been. Escape, intrigue....Now they say he's being poisoned. Dying of boredom, I'd say." She paused. "And to cap it all we've got a monster. Have you heard about our monster, Blackie? It rises out of the water at night, they say."

"A spouting whale, I'll be bound," Jack Darnell said. He lit a pipe dexterously with his good arm. "And what do we get in return for being noses for a Bow Street Runner?"

Blackstone grinned. "My word that I'll turn a blind eye to the sale of stolen liquor."

"That's mighty handsome of you," Jack Darnell said, blowing acrid smoke across the table.

"Oh, and one other thing. Make sure that my drinks aren't doctored again. If I'd drunk that rum toddy the girl brought to my room you'd have had your chance to sit on my coffin."

By the light of a candle-lantern Blackstone re-examined the knife he'd found on the floor of his room. It was light and razor-sharp and engraved on the hilt with Chinese lettering. He balanced it experimentally on his hand: a small weapon for a man the size of his assailant. Blackstone paced the room which, with the window boarded-up, felt like a cell. He undressed and went to bed and lay brooding about the attack. Attempts on his life were commonplace, but not at such an early stage in an investigation. Who wanted him dead? Certainly the French if they thought he might foil an escape plot. But other potential enemies were assembling. Jack Darnell, his daughter, Randolph Perkins; Blackstone felt that on this claustrophobic island there would soon be others. He dozed and awoke at 2 a.m. With the window blocked up, the darkness was impenetrable, tangible almost. Darkness, blackness....Then he had it: the outline of his attacker had been blurred in the darkness because the assailant was black. The first small mystery had been solved; it was a start; Blackstone slept.

CHAPTER FOUR

He was sick. And there was only one cure: escape.

Napoleon Bonaparte climbed painfully from the barouche on Deadwood plateau and surveyed the British Army encamped in the distance. Beyond them lay the ocean and the British warships which were his fetters; beyond the ships lay freedom. This morning, freedom smelled of salt air: freedom was foam-crested waves jostling their way to the American coast, freedom was gulls wheeling in the misty sky. Freedom would end the stultifying boredom; freedom would banish the nausea, fever, aching joints and the pain like a bayonet wound in his side.

Two British doctors had diagnosed hepatitis, the endemic disease on this damp, barren rock. One had been dismissed by Sir Hudson Lowe, the other court-martialled; Lowe had diagnosed malingering and wouldn't permit contradiction. Since then Napoleon's own Corsican physician, Francesco Antommarchi, had also made an official diagnosis of hepatitis and had ordered hot baths, enemas and blistering: Antommarchi's previous post had been mortician.

Napoleon stared into the grey sky. Ah, to be away from the petulant Lowe's agents who even searched women's underclothes for messages and spied upon him, an emperor, in his bath. To be away from the gossip and the miserable climate of the plateau and the snouting British guns. To be a leader of men again even if he only ruled a scrap of land in America or, perhaps, led the oppressed people of South America.

The Generals Montholon and Bertrand dismounted from the carriage and joined Napoleon. A hundred yards away stood the British orderly officer at Napoleon's residence at Longwood, Captain Englebert Lutyens, of the 20th Regiment, and half a dozen Dragoons. Right hand to his breast, Napoleon pointed out the deployment of the British forces to his two generals.

To the British observers he was merely a plump brooding man with thinning brown hair brushed forward. But at that moment Napoleon was on horseback triumphantly entering Cairo after the massacre of the Mameluke cavalry; he was storming the heights of Pratzen and cutting the Austro-Russian armies in two at Austerlitz. Then he was at Borodino with 30,000 casualties, then in retreat through the snow from Moscow. Finally he was put to rout at Waterloo so exhausted that he had to be held on his horse. The end.

"To think that it has come to this," Napoleon murmured.

"There is still hope, Your Majesty," said Charles Tristan de Montholon, the handsome and arrogant general who had once displeased Napoleon by his hasty marriage to a divorcee but had redeemed himself at Waterloo. He had pleaded to be allowed to come to St Helena because he made his commitment during the One Hundred Days – and because certain funds to which he had access were missing in France.

"Have you heard any more news?" Napoleon asked.

"Only that the ship is on the way." Montholon glanced round in case the British could hear; but they were staring at a horseman galloping across the plateau. "Everything is going according to plan."

"They'll have to be quick or they'll take a corpse through the British blockade," Napoleon said. He winced as a pain shot through his side.

General Henri Bertrand, Napoleon's aide-de-camp and formerly Grand Marshal of the Palace, said: "I'm sure you will be away from this place before the year is out, Sire." Bertrand was a timid, balding man, married to an Irish beauty, who still dreamed of the luxury of his life in the Tuileries.

Napoleon smiled bleakly. "At least I'm still tying up a handsome proportion of the British Army. Three thousand men and five hundred guns to guard the Corsican! Not to mention a general called Pine-Coffin – Pine-Coffin, I ask you – who fattens up pigs to sell to his junior officers!"

Montholon combed his curly hair with one hand. "The humiliation won't continue much longer, I promise you."

"It is the British who are humiliated," Napoleon said, massaging his side. "It is Lowe who is humiliated." Hatred rasped his voice. "To think that I have to plot against that little upstart whose only contribution to military history was to surrender Capri to the French."

"Perhaps they'll put him in front of a firing squad when you escape," Montholon suggested. "Everyone on St Helena, French and British, would declare a public holiday."

Bertrand pointed at the horseman approaching across the plateau. There were two other riders behind him. "It looks as if he's being chased," Bertrand said.

Napoleon said: "Probably some British sport. Pig-sticking, perhaps. Or perhaps they're pursuing someone accused of 'complicity with the French' – a crime worse than murder in Lowe's eyes." He shaded his eyes and stared at the horseman; and for a moment the horseman was a messenger bringing him news of a victory. "He has a good seat whoever he is." He turned to Montholon. "Your eyesight's younger than mine. What do you make of it?"

Montholon squinted into the sun burning away the mist. "Two of them are soldiers. Officers of the St Helena Regiment, I think. The man they're after is a civilian."

"Coming to assassinate me, perhaps. At least it would be a fitting end...."

"One of them's got a pistol in his hand but he doesn't look as if he's going to use it."

The British orderly officer gave an order to two of the Dragoons. They spurred their horses and galloped away to intercept the fugitive.

"Can it be anything to do with the escape?" Bertrand asked. "Can anything have gone wrong?"

"With a plan such as ours, anything could go wrong," Napoleon said. "With such audacity it can only succeed brilliantly or fail catastrophically."

They watched the five horsemen manoeuvring, the fugitive swerving suddenly and riding straight at the oncoming Dragoons as if he were jousting.

"Does he have a gun?" Napoleon asked.

"A horse-pistol at his saddle," Montholon replied. "By God but he can ride, that one."

The lone rider was past the two Dragoons, who galloped in a circle to bring up the rearguard. He reined in the horse, a big grey mare, in front of Captain Lutyens who drew his pistol. Napoleon and his generals watched with curiosity as orderly officer and horseman conferred; the horseman handed over a scroll of parchment and Lutyens slipped his pistol back in its holster.

The horseman rode over to Napoleon followed by Lutyens. The horseman dismounted, bowed and said in appalling French: "Your Majesty, I beg to introduce myself. My name is Edmund Blackstone."

Captain Lutyens, a pleasant and languid young man, the fourth official British snooper at Longwood, murmured: "Really, it's all most irregular." He turned to one of Blackstone's pursuers. "Why didn't you stop him?"

A young lieutenant of the St Helena Regiment said: "We did stop him crossing Fisher's Valley but he said he was a King's messenger and rode off like a man possessed."

"Why didn't you shoot him?" Lutyens asked mildly.

"A King's messenger, sir? And he did know the password."

Lutyens nodded. "I take your point." He unrolled the parchment and began to read.

Blackstone said: "Perhaps you would be good enough to divulge the signature and take my word for the contents."

Lutyens told the others that the signature was the King's. "But why did you gallop away from these two officers?"

Blackstone grinned. "To give them some sport. They're serving soldiers not nannies." He brushed the dust from his breeches. "This is my first full day here and already I'm being suffocated by petty restrictions. A guard every hundred yards, a gun every two hundred, passwords, curfews....Just to guard one man. With respect," he added, smiling at Napoleon.

Napoleon spoke, with Lutyens interpreting. "Have you come to see me, Monsieur Blackstone? If so, may I inquire the purpose of your visit? I normally only see visitors by appointment and then infrequently. I haven't seen Lowe for more than four years. 18 August 1816, to be precise, I called him a staff-clerk."

Blackstone was apologetic. "My mission is security." He spoke in English, attempted French, abandoned it and asked Lutyens to help. "God knows there's enough security already, but there you are. I'm a Bow Street Runner and I represent the King of England."

"Do you represent Sir Hudson Lowe, Monsieur Blackstone?"

"I can only repeat, I represent George IV of England," replied Blackstone, who hadn't yet seen Lowe.

"Bow Street Runners, eh? Their principal function, I believe, is to apprehend French spies in London."

"And to rob the thieves who rob the rich to line their own pockets if I'm not mistaken," Lutyens said.

"You'd best keep an eye on that gold watch of yours then, culley," Blackstone said.

Lutyens laughed.

"I'll say this," Napoleon said, "you cut more of a dash than most of the British in this Bastille." He looked inquiringly at Bertrand and Montholon. "What do you think, gentlemen?"

The generals indicated that it was their master's decision.

Napoleon said: "I like your style. You remind me a little of Ney, a brave man tormented by his loyalties." He noticed the surprise on Blackstone's face. "A little too near the truth to be comfortable, eh, Monsieur?"

Blackstone said: "I have never been in any doubt about Your Majesty's judgement of character."

Lutyens said: "Hey, less of the *majesty*. The Lackey doesn't like that. Sympathy with the French, my friend, is a hanging offence."

Blackstone, who had taken a liking to the placid orderly officer, said: "You seem popular enough here. Fashioning a rope for your own neck?"

"Deportation is the only punishment I yearn for," Lutyens said. "Van Diemen's Land can't be worse than this. I'll wager I'd meet a few of your friends there."

The mist had dispersed on the plateau. No one could guess what was to follow: wind, rain, hot sunshine, anything could happen with the treacherous weather on the plateau. St Helena had a climate as various as a continent and when the wind was trying to twist trees into skeins of rope at Longwood the sun would be shining in tropical Jamestown and officers would be bathing at Adjutants' Pond.

Napoleon gazed at the blue sky fleeced with clouds. "Our one good day of the year," he remarked. "Perhaps Monsieur Blackstone would be good enough to honour us with his presence at luncheon. Although," he said, hand to his side, "I doubt whether I shall eat a great deal."

Blackstone said: "I'm honoured, Your Majesty."

Longwood had been a hotch-potch of buildings, not unlike a small prison, when Napoleon first arrived. It was later extended, housing Napoleon in his own suite, some of his courtiers and their families, servants and the British orderly officer who had to confirm twice a day that he had sighted the fallen emperor. It was also a hot-house of intrigue – equalled only by Plantation House, where Sir Hudson Lowe held court – and clandestine romance involving noblemen's wives, British officers and chambermaids.

Napoleon's suite consisted of a billiards room, a drawing-room dominated by a portrait of his son, a dining-room and two private apartments. The house was built with volcanic stone and, within a couple of days, clothes hung in the cupboards had a patina of mildew; Napoleon thought the mildew had reached his soul.

The lunch to which Blackstone was invited was delicious, the cook having achieved a Gallic miracle with some broth, a few stringy chickens and atrophied vegetables washed down with white wine. Lowe always attributed

the excellence of the Longwood menu to excessive spend-
ing instead of French inventiveness; and the occasion
when Napoleon had broken up his silver plate and sold
it by auction to draw attention to the paucity of his allowance still rankled. As a result of the publicity the annual
Longwood allowance had been increased by £4,000 to
£12,000.

The ladies of the court were away visiting and lunch was
confined to Napoleon, the two generals, Blackstone and
Lutyens, who was supposed to lurk in the background and
keep his counsel.

"It's a wretched job," Lutyens confided to Blackstone. "A
fellow called Poppleton had the job first. A decent chap by
all accounts and Boney gave him a snuffbox as a reward.
Then a fellow called Blakeney of the 66th got the job. Always
searching women's underclothing for messages and drinking himself to death. Then they tried to put in an old ass
called Lyster who had served in Corsica and was obviously
hostile to Boney; Bertrand objected and won the day. After
that they appointed George Nicholls of the 66th, a decent
enough fellow but he got tired of peering through key-holes
and I got the damned job."

They ate the meal under an oak tree in the garden
where Napoleon liked to work in shirt and trousers, straw
hat and slippers.

Napoleon, at the head of the table, toyed with his food
and drank copious quantities of mineral water. "Beware,
Monsieur Blackstone," he commented, "it is common gossip – and gossip is very common on this benighted island –
that the British, or Sir Hudson Lowe rather, are trying to
poison me."

Blackstone said: "If I have to die then I would prefer it to
be eating good food."

Napoleon grunted. "They killed Cipriani," he said, refer-ring to Cipriani Franceschi, his Corsican major-domo, drunk-ard and fanatical supporter of Napoleon, who had died in 1818 after a bout of acute abdominal pains. "Odd, isn't it, that Cipriani was serving in Capri when Lowe had to surrender?"

Blackstone swallowed some chicken and drank a draught of white wine. "Your Majesty," he said, licking his lips, "I assure you that my brief is as much safeguarding your life as…"

"As what, Monsieur?"

"As ensuring that we don't have to fight another Waterloo."

Napoleon pushed his plate away. His face was grey and he held his hand to his mouth as if he might vomit. "At least," he said, "you are an honest man."

Blackstone thought: I wish you were right. And at the same time knowing that Napoleon was shrewder than that, probably knowing that he was thinking, If he's as sick as he looks then I shan't be long on St Helena. Was he being poisoned? Blackstone found himself chewing more slowly on the white breast of the chicken.

Napoleon raised his glass. "Is the meat to your taste, Monsieur?" His face was suddenly distorted with pain as if a knife had been stuck in his back. The spasm passed and he leaned back in his chair trembling.

But, even now, at the nadir of Napoleon's life, Blackstone could feel the strength of the man, the personality that had dominated rulers of nations and persuaded the most humble of men to lay down their lives for him. Blackstone dreaded his meeting with Sir Hudson Lowe; he knew that it would entail the usual confusion of allegiances: he would have to remind himself that he represented Britain and not this anxious, petty tyrant of a governor.

Napoleon pushed back his seat and stood up with difficulty. "Well, gentlemen," he said, "it's time for my dictation. If you will excuse me, Monsieur Blackstone, Captain Lutyens...." He went indoors, hand to his side.

Montholon sipped delicately at his wine. "Tell me, Monsieur Blackstone, what is the real purpose of your visit here?"

"I've told you," Blackstone said with surprise, "I've come to investigate security."

Bertrand massaged his expanding baldness. "But why a Bow Street Runner? Sir Hudson Lowe has a very able chief of police in Sir Thomas Reade. He is a most zealous man and what's more he hates the French. What more could the British ask for?"

"Actually," Lutyens said, "he's known as the Nincompoop."

"And is he one?" Blackstone asked.

"I think they mean nincomsnoop," Lutyens told him. "He collects all the gossip about Longwood at his headquarters at Alarm House. He's even arranged for an Englishwoman, married as well, to have an affair with one of Napoleon's footmen and relay all the gossip. Naturally the footman feeds her with a lot of nonsense. What appears to anger the Lackey most is any report that Napoleon is really ill. He seems to think every symptom is some sort of subterfuge."

Blackstone looked at Lutyens curiously. "Where do your sympathies really lie?"

Lutyens swallowed the last of his wine. "Really, what a question." He put down the glass. "But I know what you mean. It's difficult, very difficult. I live in the same house as the greatest military genius the world has known and I'm supposed to remain faithful to a fuss-pot."

Montholon said: "I believe there is much sympathy for the Emperor in England. I hear Lord Holland and the Duke of Sussex are seeking more human dignity for him."

Bertrand said: "The British showed how they felt at Torbay and Plymouth when His Majesty was on his way here. You would have thought it was Wellington on board the *Bellerophon*."

"Is he dictating his memoirs?" Blackstone asked.

"No, monsieur," Bertrand said, "he is probably thinking about dictating his will."

Submerged up to his neck in scalding hot water in his copper bath, Napoleon talked to Louis Marchand, his faithful, curly-haired Parisian valet who had become as much a confidant as the men of noble birth around him.

"Different from Elba, eh, Marchand?" said Napoleon, sweat sliding down his face.

Marchand shrugged. "We escaped from Elba, Your Majesty, we shall escape from here."

"It's taken the devil of a long time though. Five years or more."

"But things are different now, Your Majesty. We didn't have the means to escape then."

Napoleon looked doubtful. "What do you think as you apply fomentations and potions and emetics prescribed by that idiot of a doctor who specialised in corpses? Not quite the life you envisaged, is it, Marchand?"

"I am happy to serve," Marchand told him. "You know that, Sire."

"Yes," Napoleon said quietly, "I know that." Helped by Marchand, he heaved himself out of the bath. His clothes, including a hat with a cockade, had been laid out, but Napoleon shook his head. "I am finished for the day. Fetch my nightclothes." When Marchand brought them he said: "Did you see that man, Blackstone?"

"I saw him, Sire."

"And what did you think of him?"

"A dangerous man, Your Majesty."

"A very dangerous man," Napoleon agreed. "But I like him. I wish he worked for me. I wonder," Napoleon mused, "whether such a man could be subverted."

Marchand said: "Your Majesty, it is my belief that you could subvert Wellington himself."

"We could use a man like that in the British camp," Napoleon went on. "He could be the difference between success and failure. What do you think are his weaknesses, Marchand?"

"Women," Marchand said promptly.

"A very French observation, Marchand. But worth considering."

Napoleon went thoughtfully to bed, placed the gold watch with its chain woven from a lock of the Empress's hair beneath the pillow, and went to sleep wondering how difficult it would be to win over Edmund Blackstone, body and soul.

CHAPTER FIVE

The island was only twenty-eight miles in circumference but it encompassed the gamut of human activity.

In particular mutiny.

Wherever Blackstone travelled on his tour of inspection that afternoon he sensed mutinous feeling. It was like a prison camp in which every class of criminal from nobleman to slave has been incarcerated.

He felt it with the scarlet-coated soldiers who challenged him as he cantered along the tracks on the grey horse borrowed from Jack Darnell. They were dying like flies from dysentery and liver diseases; they were underpaid and living off starvation rations of bread, rice and salt meat; they were brutally punished by officers who sensed the undercurrent of revolt.

He felt it among sailors from the guardian ships where the off-shore heat was stifling and tropical diseases flourished. And among the Naval officers who respected a worthy but beaten opponent and expressed disgust at the treatment of Napoleon.

He felt it among some of the slaves who were given pig food to eat.

He felt it among the staff of the East India Company who had enjoyed a pleasant colonial life until the arrival of Lowe. The arrival of Lowe, Blackstone noted, never Napoleon.

He felt it at Longwood House; he felt it at Plantation House.

And, because mutiny is contagious, he felt it among every householder, shop-keeper, fisherman and whore in Jamestown.

Blackstone explored most of the island, crossing the morose plateau to the mountains and valleys where passion flower, bougainvillea and crimson canna took the sun beside the sea. With such extremes of climate, he thought, it was a wonder anyone survived.

He visited Sandy Bay and Rupert's Bay, the two points at opposite ends of the island where the "monster" had been sighted. Then he went back to the Good Neighbour to change and pay his respects – or disrespects – to the Governor.

But first he met Captain Randolph Perkins, who was waiting for him in the parlour of the tavern. "Ah," Blackstone said, "there you are. How about a glass of sherry?"

"Sherry be damned," Perkins snapped. He looked very handsome in his uniform – scarlet coat with silver lace edging, sword at his side, black shako with white plume and gold and crimson cords under his arm. But something not quite right, Blackstone reaffirmed; some in-breeding, perhaps, in the noble features; ostentation in the jewelled fingers to compensate for some insecurity.

"Just as you please," Blackstone said, sitting down and stretching his long legs which ached after his long absence from the saddle. "Lucy, a glass of contraband sherry, my love." He looked inquiringly at Perkins. "Are you quite sure?"

"Where were you?" Perkins demanded. He put his shako on the table and remained standing, muscles working on the line of his jaw.

"Where was I when?"

"At eleven this morning, dammit."

Blackstone sipped his sherry. "Let me think. I do believe I was somewhere near the farm of a lady called Miss Mason who, I'm told, rides a bullock. Very eccentric we English." He put down his glass. "Yes, that's where I was, I remember looking at my watch." Blackstone took his gold Breguet from his pocket.

"I told you to report to my lodgings."

" 'Pon my soul," Blackstone exclaimed, "I quite forgot."

"You had no business to forget. And you've no business to adopt this attitude."

"Why's that?" Blackstone asked.

"Because I am in charge of the investigation into the security of St Helena."

"Does Sir Hudson Lowe know that?"

"I have already discussed the situation with Sir Hudson. He understands my position perfectly."

"Good for him," Blackstone said. He rolled the sherry round his mouth. "A nice drop this, Lucy. Boney must have helped himself during the Peninsular War."

"And what have you been doing, pray? Acquainting yourself with the local strumpets?"

"I thought that was an instrument you played," Blackstone said, staring into the amber depths of his glass and adding: "No, as a matter of fact I've been talking to someone who should concern us far more than the Governor."

"Someone more important than Sir Hudson Lowe?"

"Name of Napoleon Bonaparte. That is the arch-cove we're trying to stop escaping, isn't it?"

"You had no right...."

"Every right," Blackstone interrupted. He took the letter from George IV from his pocket. "Read that, culley."

"I have a letter from the King giving me full authority...."

"Over military security. Yes, I've no doubt. This letter gives me authority to take whatever steps I think necessary in civilian matters. I don't think even poor old Boney considers himself to be in the army any longer."

Perkins handed back the letter, the dying sunlight catching the gems on his fingers.

"I shall report this to Sir Hudson Lowe."

"I should if I were you. As a matter of fact I've sent my first message back to London on the brig that sailed this afternoon."

Blackstone marvelled at his ability to lie spontaneously and outrageously, a legacy from his youth as a stock buzzer, as they called handkerchief thieves, when an elderly gentleman had you by the ear with a fine piece of white silk in your hand. He wasn't proud of this talent. Nor was he sure why he reacted so malevolently to Perkins; neither of them could help what they were.

Perkins's features tightened. Now, Blackstone thought, we shall know the calibre of the man. The effete manner had vanished: Perkins was snarling. "You really know the tricks of the gutter, don't you. The tricks of the gutter where you were spawned."

"We didn't run to gutters in the Rookery," Blackstone said.

Perkins drew back, removed one white glove and made to slap Blackstone round the face.

Blackstone held up his hand. "Nor did we run to gloves in the Rookery. It strikes me as a rather childish gesture from a man announcing his intention of killing another. Shall we say dawn, whenever that is in this God-forsaken place? I leave the choice of weapons to you."

"Very well." Perkins replaced the glove. "I suggest Rupert's Bay. Is that acceptable to you?"

"Quite acceptable. That's where they saw the monster, I believe."

Perkins gave a pantomime click of his heels and walked out into the scented dusk.

Lucinda Darnell said: "Now you've done it, haven't you?"

"I've done it all right."

"Was it really necessary? I mean you deliberately provoked him."

"He deserved it."

"But why, Blackie? I mean, all right, he's a pompous ass but he can't help that. Now one of you's going to get killed." Her voice softened. "There's no sense in it, is there, Blackie?"

Blackstone handed her his empty glass and agreed that there wasn't.

She re-filled the glass. "There isn't another reason, is there? They say his wife is a very attractive woman. I know you of old, Edmund Blackstone."

"No other reason," Blackstone said.

"Isn't it against the law to fight a duel?" She thought about it. "Surely you should be preventing duels not starting them?"

"They shouldn't take guttersnipes from the Rookery and make them Bow Street Runners."

She rattled her ear-rings, which this evening were tiny gold cages with a ruby in one and an emerald in the other. "That's no answer and you know it."

"Ah, Lucy, you're a hard woman." Which was the last thing she looked, he decided, with her green eyes anxious and her ringlets soft in the glow of the lanterns.

She said: "I wouldn't want anything to happen to you, Blackie."

"Me, the man who betrayed you?"

"You didn't betray us. I know that. So does Jack." She drank from his glass. "Nor would I want anything to happen to Captain Perkins. He's a handsome man and there aren't too many around these parts."

"So you think I might be killed?"

"One of you will."

"Then what about granting the wish of a half condemned man, Lucy?"

"No," she said firmly.

What have I done? Blackstone pondered. More importantly, why? Pomposity in a man was no excuse to set the stage to kill him. It's my background, he decided, as he shaved in the tin mirror on the wall of his room. Inferiority? Superiority? Anyway, the cross I shall bear for the rest of my life – if I'm not killed at dawn.

Whatever the outcome of the duel I'm finished, he thought. Dead or disgraced. An end to his career on the right side of the law and back to the other dark side; the side, perhaps, where it had been written that he should dwell if a kindly benefactor hadn't interfered with destiny and rescued him.

He dressed carefully, as always, in the blue swallow-tail coat and white shirt and looked at himself in the mirror. The tin distorted his features, imparting brutality. Or was it distortion? God knows. We are our parents' seeds.

He traced the line from nose to mouth, felt the rasp of shaven bristles, touched the hollows in his cheeks, moulded in starving youth and never to be filled in.

He shrugged, slipped the French stiletto in his boot, tested the cocking mechanism of the Manton, and blew out the candle-lantern.

I should have been a highwayman, he thought.

And with that he departed to meet the Governor of St Helena.

CHAPTER SIX

Sir Hudson Lowe, Lieutenant-General, Knight Commander of the Most Honourable Order of the Bath, Russian Cross of St George, Prussian Military Order of Merit, Governor and Commander-in-Chief of St Helena, was angry. More angry than usual.

He sat in his study with his *aide-de-camp*, Major Gideon Gorrequer, brooding about the disloyalty and subversion around him.

The French were up to something. His spies had reported a new confidence in their camp which was a contradiction of Napoleon's alleged state of health; but they hadn't come up with anything definite and had probably been seduced by the French charm which Sir Hudson found elusive. He had once tried to establish a dignified relationship with Napoleon but had been rebuffed and publicly humiliated; since then Bonaparte had waged a war of attrition against him as remorselessly as a Grand Army campaign.

The Navy snubbed him; the Army was mutinous; the civilians blamed him for the lack of decent food (although the French seemed to manage well enough); there was Liberal agitation in Britain for a better deal for his captive; and his wife was drinking too much.

"But when they get their invitations to a reception at Plantation House they all come running, eh, Gorrequer?"

"*They,* Your Excellency?" queried the smooth-faced aide with the mocking eyes who every night wrote up his private diary in which he referred to Lowe as Mach (Machiavelli) and Lady Lowe as Sultana.

"All of them," Lowe said. "Every single ungrateful upstart on this island. They all come trotting up the drive as eager as hounds at the hunt when they hear the Governor is entertaining."

Gorrequer smiled at the small sandy man dressed up in his lieutenant-general's uniform for tonight's reception. "They are only human, Your Excellency." He had once thought of writing a biography about his master but had discarded the idea because the material was too thin.

Lowe, born in the same year as Napoleon, had fought in Egypt with the Corsican Rangers, undertaken some intelligence work – confirming Gorrequer's opinion of military intelligence – surrendered to the French at Capri, faced Napoleon at the indecisive battle of Bautzen, taken part in sundry other campaigns, carried the news of the fall of Paris to London, accepted a post as British quartermaster-general in Holland, landed at Marseilles after Waterloo and finally been dispatched – banished, Gorrequer thought – to St Helena.

Wellington reportedly thought Lowe was a fool; Gorrequer had always admired Wellington's judgement.

Lowe recalled the reason for his latest spasm of anger. "Now it seems that they don't trust me to safeguard Bonaparte."

"*They,* Your Excellency?"

"The King, as yet uncrowned, has sent two men to investigate the security of St Helena. Really, it's too bad."

Gorrequer smiled. "Ah yes, the two new arrivals. They are, I believe, attending the reception tonight."

"One of them's a whippersnapper called Perkins from the Grenadiers. I met him this morning. The other's some wretched thief-catcher who hasn't even had the good manners to present himself. Fellow called Blackstone. He seems to be an errand boy for young Perkins." Lowe stood up and paced the room, stroking the braid on his new uniform. "Perkins seems a decent enough young chap. Not his fault that he's been chosen for this job."

"The errand boy seems to have been delivering messages already, Your Excellency." Gorrequer coughed to disguise his laughter.

"Messages? What messages?"

"It seems he called upon General Bonaparte this morning."

Lowe's face paled and it seemed to Gorrequer that his freckles performed a war-dance. He hit the desk with his fist. "He called upon Bonaparte?"

Gorrequer nodded.

"He shall answer for this," Lowe said. "By God he'll answer for it."

They heard a crunch of wheels outside.

"Your Excellency," Gorrequer murmured, "your guests are starting to arrive."

"Oh yes," Lowe said to himself, "he'll answer for it all right."

The reception was held in the ground-floor drawing-rooms of Plantation House, a substantial twenty-four-room mansion set amid lawns and trees. An English squire's house given airs by the Union Jack flying above it.

Guests were received in the hall and introduced to Sir Hudson and Lady Lowe before circulating beneath the chandeliers, taking sherry and discussing the Neighbour, the privations and scandal of the island.

Perkins and his wife were hovering in the background when Blackstone arrived.

The Governor held Blackstone's hand for a moment. "A word with you later in private," he said.

Lady Lowe, heavily rouged and slightly drunk, smiled lopsidedly at Blackstone. "Good evening, Mr Blackstone," she said, tongue searching for the words, "you are a welcome addition to our little community."

Blackstone bowed and joined the Perkins.

They took drinks from a silver tray carried by a liveried footman and returned to a corner. "Now," Louise said, violet, slightly-crossed eyes accusing, "what's all this I hear about a duel?"

Blackstone sipped his sherry; it tasted the same as the Good Neighbour's brew. "Whatever you heard I'm sure it was correct," he said.

"You shouldn't be so impetuous." Blackstone watched the mole moving at her bosom. "You must make it up." A little too much emphasis on the *must*, Blackstone thought.

"It's a question of honour, ma'am," Blackstone said. "There's very little we can do about it."

"Honour, my foot." The violet eyes seemed to darken. "Do you realise this will ruin both of you?"

Blackstone shrugged. What she meant, he thought, was that it would ruin her.

Louise turned to her husband. "Weren't you going to say something?"

Perkins, looking like a melting waxwork in his dress uniform, mopped sweat from his face with a red and gold handkerchief. Blackstone's fingers twitched: it was the sort of kingsman he would have yearned to pinch in his youth.

"Well?" Blackstone prompted.

"It's nothing." A prince in an operetta who had forgotten his lines.

Louise said quietly: "You promised me." There was a cutting-edge to her voice which Blackstone hadn't noticed before.

"We've been talking it over...." Perkins began.

"And you want to call it off?" Blackstone regarded him with surprise. Undefined weakness, he had suspected; but not cowardice.

"It's like this...."

"Then you must apologise."

"No." Perkins mopped away at his burning face.

Louise said to Blackstone: "Please, Blackie, don't you realise that what Randolph is doing takes courage."

Blackstone, who thought Perkins should be wearing a yellow uniform, said: "What exactly is he doing?"

She moved closer to Blackstone. He could smell her perfume. "If you have a duel tomorrow then both of you are finished. It will be impossible to fight without being seen by the soldiers who are dotted around like a rash of scarlet fever. Randolph will be court-martialled.... God knows what will happen to you."

"You seem to forget that one of us will most probably be killed."

She made a gesture with her fan as if that were of small importance. Death rather than dishonour! "All Randolph is doing is asking for a postponement."

"Randolph seems to me to be doing very little."

Perkins tossed back his sherry as if it were whisky. "I propose that we settle this question of honour at the first possible occasion at Leicester Fields on our return to England. I feel that won't be long in view of the state of health of General Bonaparte." He examined a diamond sparkling on his forefinger.

Did it really matter? Blackstone wondered. Honour. What the hell was honour? Perkins was an accomplished duellist, he was a marksman and a fair swordsman. He had always considered the macabre formalities of duels ludicrous when he had been dispatched to break them up. He favoured a duel with fists on a green field spotted with blood, the loser the first man who couldn't rise. Duelling was stylised, foppish murder.

But, at the moment, the thing was to escape from this sickening conversation.

"Very well," Blackstone snapped. "Your apology is accepted. Leicester Fields be it. By the way," he added, "I believe this is yours." He handed Perkins the watch he had taken from the pickpocket in Brighton. "I hope you keep a closer watch on Boney than you did that."

He was halfway across the drawing-room to introduce himself to Lieutenant-Colonel Sir Thomas Reade, deputy governor and chief of police – the Nincompoop – when he spotted the Negro. He was dressed in scarlet livery handing silver trays of drinks to senior footmen. He was a huge man with an ebony face and one arm hanging loosely at his side.

Blackstone felt the knife tear into flesh, heard the window shattering.

He went up to the Negro. "What have you done to your arm, culley?"

The Negro didn't reply.

"I asked you a question."

The Negro shook his head, eyes staring at Blackstone.

A Chinese footman took Blackstone's arm. "You won't get any sense out of him, sir," he said. "They took his tongue out ten years ago." His voice was shy and fragile.

"What for?"

"For making improper suggestions to the lady of the house, sir."

For rejecting her advances more like, Blackstone thought.

Sir Hudson Lowe walked across the room. "I'd like to see you now, Mr Blackstone. In my study. It will only take a few moments. Then," he said acidly, "you can return to the servants."

"Just a minute, sir," Blackstone said. He turned. But the Negro had vanished.

Blackstone had hired a sleek black Arab stallion in place of the grey mare he had exhausted during the day and he rode it now from the lights and laughter of Plantation House towards the toytown of Jamestown. He held the horse tightly with his thighs, recalling the fear that had crossed the face of the black servant, a fear you could almost smell. And then the Negro had vanished. Blackstone had questioned the other servants but no one knew where he had gone to; only that he had once worked for an eccentric Englishman called Mullins. Blackstone rode the horse fiercely to purge himself of the lassitude that had overcome him ever since he was given the assignment in Brighton; now the boredom had increased tenfold since his introduction to the exiled gossip-mongers of St Helena. He understood Napoleon's decay: he would have degenerated into a jelly within a year. The frustration was already affecting his attitudes; there had been no need to provoke Perkins into a duel, no need for his discourtesy to Lowe, who was merely an inept man dutifully trying to perform a job too big for him.

Lowe had pulled at his thin nose as if he was trying to remove it, furrowed his thick sandy eyebrows and blustered about disloyalty and lack of discipline. Finally, like a husband seeking some sort of sick satisfaction from his wife's confession of adultery, he had asked: "And so, Mr Blackstone, what did you think of our prisoner?"

Blackstone said: "I think he's being poisoned."

It had been right between the eyes. "Poisoned? Are you a lunatic as well as an uncouth lout with the flavour of the stews in your voice? Poisoned, man? What in the name of God gave you that idea? The man's shamming, anyone can see that." And he had launched into a tirade about Blackstone falling for Napoleon's wiles just like every other gullible visitor who had returned to England and campaigned for leniency for Bonaparte.

Blackstone stopped him. "His symptoms are not unlike those of arsenic poisoning," he said mildly.

"And what are those, pray?"

"Faintness, nausea, brown vomit, a burning in the throat, intense thirst, abdominal pains, eyelids puffy. At lunch today the Emperor—"

"General."

"—the General displayed some of those symptoms. Not conclusive, of course, but we have to remember that the servant Cipriani Franceschi died of acute abdominal pains which could have been attributable to poison. I believe he was at Capri at the same time as yourself, Sir Hudson."

"Are you suggesting I had anything to do with Cipriani's death?" Lowe tapped the desk with well-manicured fingers.

"I'm merely remarking on the coincidence. This island is full of coincidences. I believe Wellington once stayed here."

"Watch your tongue, Mr Blackstone," Lowe said, a hiss to his voice. "It could hang you. Now, sir, why did you take it upon yourself to visit Bonaparte without permission and evade the horse patrols?"

Blackstone handed him the letter from George IV, adding that his job was testing security and if he, one man, could reach Napoleon without being caught then he didn't think much of it. "Incidentally," Blackstone lied, "the King gave me full permission to visit Napoleon without an escort. My last employment was bodyguard to His Majesty," he added lazily, taking some snuff from the warm gold box.

Lowe flung the letter across the desk. He had a defeated look about him and Blackstone was about to restore some of his pride when they were interrupted by Lady Lowe, who entered the study with a hiccup.

Spurring his horse, Blackstone saw ahead of him the flickering lights of Jamestown and, beyond them, the lanterns of the watchdog ships. He guided the horse towards Rupert's Bay because he didn't believe that the monster was a figment of any slave's imagination; he believed that something existed and that, whatever it was, it had a purpose, perhaps to distract attention from some other operation. Such as an escape.

He waited on a hillside overlooking the moonlit sea for two hours. But nothing stirred beyond a cutter returning to a brig, a few fish flopping and the waves slapping against the rocks.

Finally he rose, legs aching, and rode into Jamestown thinking about the Negro. Whatever the plan was – poisoning, escape or merely some island vendetta which someone had feared Blackstone might spoil – the Negro held the key, or at least a small twist of it.

He tethered the horse in the stables and made his way along the passage of the sleeping tavern. He was tired and chilled by the moisture of the night. Without bothering to light the candle-lantern he tugged off his boots, discarded the rest of his clothes and slipped between the sheets.

The body beside him in the bed was big and well-muscled and already growing cold and Blackstone knew that he had found the Negro and that he would never be of any use to him.

CHAPTER SEVEN

Next day, after the tongueless body of the Negro had been laid out in the over-populated mortuary between a soldier who had died of liver disease and a sailor who had died of dysentery, Blackstone decided to find himself a servant.

He found Number Nine.

The duties of Number Nine were to polish his Hoby boots, press his Weston coats and trousers and Levantine silk shirts with the fluted frill down the centre; to trim his hair, to run errands and to organise a spy network among the island's servants; always, in Blackstone's experience, the most efficient network of all. On St Helena it had one disadvantage: the servants were so accustomed to being paid by various masters for information that they tended to invent what they couldn't discover.

Number Nine was a fragile little coolie with a sparrow's voice and eyes yellowed from opium smoking. He was one of the 481 Chinese on the island and he had helped to build a pavilion in the grounds of Longwood, where much of the gardening was done by Chinese supervised by Napoleon. He spoke fluted English, threw razor-sharp axes with terrifying accuracy and was utterly faithful to the master who paid him the most money.

Blackstone briefed him while he snipped his hair with a pair of scissors with elaborate silver handles. He told him he wanted dossiers on the activities of leading members of Napoleon's household and servants close to him; in particular, Blackstone told the little man fluttering round him, he wanted information about Dr Francesco Antommarchi, Napoleon's personal physician.

Because, Blackstone admitted to himself, I am more interested in the possibility that Napoleon is being poisoned than the possibility that he is planning to escape.

The Chinaman stopped snipping, ran an ivory comb through the strong black hair and held the tin mirror in front of Blackstone. Blackstone surveyed his handiwork, nodded approvingly and gave Number Nine a gold sovereign; it was, he reflected, the most expensive haircut of his life.

The identity of the Negro was established as Sebastian. He had been hired for the one evening for the Governor's reception. Death was due to garrotting, the wire having cut through the wind-pipe like a knife. Conventional strangulation, it was pointed out, would have taken too long because the tongue assists suffocation and the late Sebastian was not in a position to assist his murderer. A knife-wound slicing the length of the huge right bicep was also found.

The superintendent of St Helena police, Sir Thomas Reade, who was also deputy-governor, wasn't pleased about the murder. Nor was he pleased about the presence of a Bow Street Runner on his tight little island. He made his views known in his bluff manner which, Blackstone suspected, masked a sly and ruthless intriguer. The obvious suspect, Reade told Blackstone with a laugh, was Blackstone himself. The Negro had made a second attempt to burgle Blackstone's room and Blackstone had killed him. Blackstone should be thankful it was only a black slave who had died, Reade hinted; otherwise it might be a hanging case at Rupert's Bay where the scaffold overlooked the deep grave of the Atlantic. Not a very auspicious start to Blackstone's investigation, was it?

Blackstone said: "The new king is most concerned that the new laws concerning slaves be implemented. I shall convey your views on the value of their lives to him."

The smile on Reade's chubby features remained but his eyes were as benign as an alligator's. "*If* you ever return to England, Mr Blackstone," he said.

How many enemies was it possible to make in one week? Blackstone wondered.

He left the inquest and walked into the parlour of the Good Neighbour for a dog's nose. Not a drink for sweltering Jamestown; but a nostalgic drink with the cries of London trapped in its depths. "Rosemary and lavender." "Pretty pins, pretty women." Winter setting in and moths of snow on the evening air; horses' hooves on cobbles and the warm breath of the taverns; beefsteak and oyster sauce washed down with stout in the Brown Bear across the road from Bow Street headquarters; the new gas-light in the Dials illuminating its clock with seven dials; a twopenny hop at a dancehall with fiddle, harp, cornopean and a flushed, flirtatious girl in your arms; hot pies, potatoes in their jackets and chestnuts roasting on the street stalls. Blackstone licked his lips.

He sipped his drink, isolated among the boozy bluejackets and soldiers, and remembered the last case he had handled before starting his Royal stint which every Runner hated.

He had been supping a tankard of ale in the Brown Bear when a constable had come dashing in with the news that an elephant had escaped from a menagerie along the Strand through Exeter Change Bazaar. Blackstone and Ruthven had gone along, partly as Runners, partly for the sport. When they got there they found a roped-off crowd staring at Prinny, a five-year-old Bombay elephant, at bay facing a firing squad of scarlet-jacketed soldiers. With his trunk the elephant had torn aside oak bars three feet wide, killed one keeper and injured another. They had given him poisoned food but Prinny had rejected it. Now he was to be executed.

Blackstone had turned away as volley after volley crashed out. It was said that 152 balls were fired into the elephant's back and still it didn't fall. Finally, when it fell to its knees, they pierced its heart with a sabre attached to the end of a crowbar.

Blackstone, who had lived all his life with death and cruelty, had come nearer to vomiting than ever before.

The memory was enough to jerk him back to this imitation English tavern in another world. A mulatto girl came and sat at his table; nose flat, eyes dark, hair neither wiry nor sleek but well brushed, breasts firm and brown beneath the low-cut cotton dress printed with bright flowers and hemmed with tassels like a curtain.

She smiled at him, teeth very white and slightly splayed. "What you think about?" she asked.

Blackstone smiled at her. "An elephant," he said.

She looked puzzled. "Please?"

"Never you mind. Leave a man alone with his thoughts."

"You no like jig-jig?"

"I like it very much. But not just now."

She sighed. "I like to jig-jig with you. You let me know when you want. Maybe I do it for free."

And maybe you won't, Blackstone thought as she flounced away. But he had been a long time without a woman. It doesn't say much for your virility, he mused, when your only bedmate has been a corpse.

His eyes wandered to Lucinda Darnell, dispensing drinks while a whore with a wooden leg, very popular by all accounts, bargained with two off-duty pickets from the 66th Regiment. Thoughtfully, he ordered another dog's nose.

In his room, as dusk thickened into dark soup outside, Blackstone considered the oral reports brought to him by Number Nine, sifting the truth from the embroidery. Blackstone hadn't given him another sovereign, not yet; never spoil the market.

Most of the information he knew already. Montholon was outwardly the most dangerous inhabitant at Longwood. An ambitious adventurer trapped like a sleek cat, willing to chance anything to escape; Bertrand, the most senior of the entourage, seemed too timid to lead desperados, which is what they would be – although he might be a willing accomplice. It wouldn't be the first time Blackstone had been deceived by appearances. He recalled a mild-mannered chandler from Bow Street who had threatened to kill himself; instead of killing himself the chandler had tried to knife his wife and had injured two constables, biting one of their fingers to the bone. No, you couldn't dismiss Bertrand.

But could anyone escape from this place? Napoleon had once said: "This is a disgraceful land. It is a prison." But it was more than a prison; it was a dungeon that had erupted from the ocean. No one could escape the spies, pickets, cannons and the ships, two constantly circling the island. There were only a couple of possible landing or disembarking points apart from Jamestown and they were bristling with fortifications. The idea was ridiculous, a figment of Lowe's fevered imagination. Napoleon had been here for five years. Why hadn't he tried before? Why had he left it until he was desperately sick?

Or being poisoned?

Blackstone considered what the Chinaman had told him about Dr Francesco Antommarchi. He had been sent to the island in 1819 on a salary of 9,000 francs a year, a paltry sum for a skilled physician, but not for a butcher. A man trained to dissect cadavers sent to administer to a dethroned emperor? Again Blackstone sensed the dead hand of Lowe.

What did the rest of the Napoleonic camp think of Antommarchi? Not much, according to Number Nine. He seemed to have one cure: enemas. Blackstone thought it was the British who were obsessed with their bowels. Now, apparently, he was contemplating tartaric emetics which could only cause the patient further agonies.

Who in that faithful band of Frenchmen would want to poison their God? Unless, Blackstone thought, poison was being infiltrated into Longwood by the British. There wasn't a Briton on the island who didn't want these siege conditions to end; the newcomers wanted to go home, the original residents wanted an end to the petty tyranny of their occupation. This could only happen if the Neighbour were to die.

The other servant interested Blackstone. Marchand. But he was an enigma, his loyalty impenetrable even to Number Nine and his soft-footed spies.

Antommarchi and Marchand. Blackstone filed their names in his brain.

He glanced at his Breguet. 7.50 p.m. Lucinda Darnell would be finishing her toilet prior to the evening's work in the parlour.

Perhaps, Blackstone thought as he washed and put on a clean white Levantine silk shirt, she wouldn't mind being late for once.

❧ ❧ ❧

He knocked firmly on her door and when she asked who it was he told her: "It's the flasherman. I have a message for you."

Lucinda Darnell opened the door slightly. Her red hair was tousled as if she were halfway through combing it and Blackstone could see that she was in her chemise.

She said: "I can guess what the message is, Blackie. The answer's still no."

Blackstone pushed the door gently and it gave a little. "I was sitting in my room," he said, "thinking of those other nights. We always seem to be together with the sound of waves close by, don't we, Lucy?"

"You're a romantic devil, Blackie, when you choose to be. And a hard bastard when you choose."

Blackstone grinned. "No reason why the two shouldn't go together."

"But you're on the wrong side of the law for me, Blackie."

"I've brought some champagne," Blackstone said. "You always had a taste for champagne as I recall it. Do you remember when you used to bring a bottle on to the red cliffs of Devon?"

"Champagne? Where the hell did you get that from? I haven't tasted it for ages."

"A small Chinese friend of mine pinched it from Napoleon Bonaparte." He pushed the door a little harder. "Just a chat about old times" – his voice lingered over the words – "over a glass of the best French champagne in the world."

"I don't know...."

He caught the hesitation. "Just a chat. Nothing more. I promise."

"Very well. Just let me put some clothes on."

It seemed to Blackstone to be an unnecessary precaution but he waited patiently in the passage.

The champagne cork went off like a bullet and Blackstone quickly poured the foaming liquid into two glasses. "To the past," he said, clinking glasses and thinking, To the immediate future.

"You're very sure of yourself, aren't you, Blackie," she said, sipping the champagne appreciatively.

"Not really," Blackstone replied truthfully. "I'm never sure about myself these days, not since I became honourable and started carrying a baton with a gilt crown on it instead of a cudgel weighted with lead."

They were sitting at a table scattered with combs, brushes and pots of face-powder. She was wearing a long, wine-coloured dress loosely fastened at the breast. The champagne and the intimacy of the scene coalesced. He poured more champagne.

After a while she asked him if there was a chance that he might return to the right side of the law; by which she meant the wrong side.

"There's always a chance. Many people say the Runners are no better than the villains they chase. There's a lot of truth in that and it's very confusing. Set a thief to catch a thief. It's the hypocrisy of it that upsets me." He leaned forward, looking into her green eyes. "I'm sorry about your father, Lucy. I really am."

"I know it," she said.

More champagne frothed in the glasses. Outside the cicadas started their music and they could hear the wash of the sea. A moth flirted with the lantern hanging on the wall.

Then the champagne was finished and he was on his feet, saying, "Well, I really must be going. A man of my word, you see." She looked surprised.

She stood up and he knocked over a glass and she was in his arms and he was kissing her with the months of abstinence about to terminate.

Half an hour later, laying naked beside him, red hair spread beneath her face, green eyes half closed, she reminded him about his promise that he had only come to talk about old times.

"That's the trouble with being a Bow Street Runner," he told her. "I'm a hypocrite."

He touched her fine breasts and felt their pink tips come to life again. She touched the scars on his body. "Such a hard body," she murmured. "Such a tough, hard hypocrite." Her nails ran down his back.

For a moment they listened to the waves. "Always the sea," he said, leaning over her.

The moth flirted too dangerously with the lantern on the wall and fell to the floor with scorched wings.

CHAPTER EIGHT

The "monster" surfaced at 1.55 a.m. in the fishing grounds beyond Bird Island and Egg Island. The sea was calm, which was the way this particular "monster" liked it, and moonlight lay in a broad avenue leading to the horizon.

The officer in charge of the look-out post on Bird Island had rowed ashore half an hour earlier and made his way through the coastal mountains, crossed Old Woman's Valley and kept an assignation in Lemon Garden with a girl who lived in the cluster of farms near Thomson's Wood. His dalliance lasted another half an hour, then he made his way back, smoothing the creases from his uniform. He was a little intoxicated.

The rest of his men were totally drunk after an unexpected gift of a cask of brandy from the French. At 1.56 one of the red-coats walked unsteadily to the edge of the rock to urinate. Staring out to sea, he saw a black object pushing aside the ocean, silver water streaming down its flanks. The redcoat regarded it mistily, shaded his eyes with one hand and found that he was urinating over his boots.

He called out to the other soldiers lolling around the half-empty cask in the moonlight. "Look." Buttoning himself up with one hand, he pointed out to sea with the other.

An Irish soldier joined him. "What?"

"That," said the first soldier impatiently.

"Bejaysus," exclaimed the second soldier. "What is it?"

"I don't know, Paddy. Tell me, am I drunk?"

"As a bastard," the Irishman confirmed.

"Are you drunk?"

"As two bastards," the Irishman said.

"Can you see what I can see?"

"I think I can see what you see. But then I don't know what you can see." He shivered. "But, by all that's Holy, I don't like the looks of it. Where's the lieutenant?"

"Having it away," the first soldier said. "Firing his cannon, the lucky sod."

"We'd better tell him," the Irishman said.

"Except," said the first soldier, "that he's taken the bloody boat."

Out at sea the "monster" turned slowly in the water, its mouth gaping open. The look-out on the crow's nest of H.M.S. *Racoon* saw the mouth, moaned softly to himself and relayed an incoherent message to the decks. The captain was roused and came on to the bridge with his telescope. His eyesight was bad – a fact not known to the Admiralty – and he decided that it was a whale.

On Bird Island Lieutenant Fairfax moored the dinghy with difficulty and rejoined his men. He felt tired and replete and his head was still singing to the accompaniment of the brandy. He felt excessively fond of his men; he admired their cameraderie and loyalty and intended to tell them so.

He found them staring out to sea. He joined them and decided that an attempt to rescue Napoleon was underway. He was pleased with his perspicacity and determined to be decisive as well. "Fire the cannon," he said, helping himself to a nip of brandy. "Sink it with one ball, my boys."

The cannon swivelled and raised its heavy muzzle.

"On target?" Lieutenant Fairfax demanded.

"On target, sir."

"Fire," Lieutenant Fairfax shouted joyfully, feeling the medal being pinned on his tunic, assessing his place in history.

The cannon fired; cliffs and sea were suffused with red and gold light. The explosion hurt the soldiers' eardrums, sent flocks of gulls soaring towards the stars, finally lost itself in echoes down the valleys of St Helena.

Lieutenant Fairfax shaded his eyes.

H.M.S. *Racoon* shuddered slightly as the ball hit her amidships. A gunpowder keg exploded and the ship began to burn fiercely.

Lieutenant Fairfax looked for the "monster" but it had disappeared.

His place in history now assured, he poured himself another tot of brandy.

Lucinda Darnell had decided not to work that evening and Blackstone left her room at 1 a.m. The tavern was deserted, the parlour in darkness.

Somewhere he heard a sound. Footsteps. But coming from beneath him.

He went into the moonlit parlour; the sound was plainer. Footsteps moving with measured tread as though someone were pacing a room.

But what room? The cellars were at the back of the tavern, and beneath the parlour there were presumably only the foundations on which the inn had been built.

Glancing around the pale outlines of the parlour, Blackstone experienced the curious sensation that assails everyone from time to time that he had been in these exact circumstances before. But, on this occasion, the sensation was too strong to be a trick of the mind. I have been here alone in the moonlight before, he thought.

He shivered.

One hand found the warm butt of his pistol, the other felt for the stiletto.

I have been in this parlour at this precise time with the moonlight shining through the lattice windows, the smell of stale beer on the air, a rat scuttering across the floor, footsteps pacing beneath me.

But, unless he had been sleep-walking, it couldn't have happened here.

Stealthily, Blackstone walked across the room and sat at the table where the mulatto had accosted him and listened. The footsteps were directly beneath him.

If it wasn't here then where was it that this had all happened before. Was it the champagne? Had his mind been deranged by making love so passionately after months alone in bed and hammock?

The footsteps stopped. A chair grated. Silence. A clock ticking in the parlour with exaggerated sound. The tiny sounds of the mystified rat returning to investigate this nocturnal intruder sitting at the table.

Another scrape and the footsteps started again. Right beneath him. Blackstone knelt and put his ear to the floorboards; the noise became louder.

At the same time he smelled oil. The smell was strongest at the foot of two of the legs of the table. He stood up and gently pulled at the table top. The whole table rose on oiled joints screwed into the floor.

Then Blackstone remembered.

The interior of the Good Neighbour was a facsimile of the Mount Pleasant Inn at Dawlish Warren where he had first met Lucinda Darnell and her brigand of a father. That was where he had stood in the moonlight and listened to stealthy movements beneath the floorboards as the smugglers stacked Hollands and Cognac in the caverns hollowed in red sandstone.

Blackstone guessed that, at the end of the tunnel which had opened at his feet, there would be similar caverns concealing liquor stolen from the French or smuggled from merchant ships plying the Atlantic.

He stared into the dark mouth of the tunnel. It smelled of damp and rats and alcohol. He debated whether to take a lantern. But why illuminate the target for the man with the restless footsteps?

Cautiously he stepped into the darkness on to a slippery flight of stone steps. He thought he discerned a faint glow in the distance; but it might have been his imagination. The steps curved round a damp wall. Ahead of him ran an army of rats; he heard a splash as one fell into water somewhere below the steps.

Then he was on flat ground with water running beside him to the sea. He took the Manton from his pocket and cocked it. Now there was definitely a glow ahead. A breeze fanned his cheeks and he could smell the sea.

He reached the penumbra of the darkness. There was no sound except the gurgle of the water. Hugging the wall of the tunnel, he moved further into the dim light. The rats had vanished into their dark homes; he thought he heard breathing. Peering round a sharp corner of the wall, Blackstone stared into a cave with recesses in the walls stacked with casks and barrels.

But it wasn't the contraband that caught Blackstone's attention. Made his mind reel. Made him wonder if the champagne had been poisoned or had deranged his mind.

Standing in the middle of the cave, right hand to his breast, was a plump figure with a sallow face, thinning brown hair brushed forward, staring out through an aperture in the wall as if he were watching the progress of a battle.

The scene registered briefly in Blackstone's mind before it was extinguished by darkness as a heavy object crashed on to the back of his head and he fell into the water flowing into the sea.

CHAPTER NINE

L e Petit Caporal, as Napoleon had been nicknamed by his
troops, rose at 7 a.m., determined, despite his discomfort, to revert to his old routine. He called for Marchand,
slipped into fustian trousers, white piqué dressing gown and
red morocco slippers.

He drank some tea while Marchand prepared his toilet and surveyed the small room, facing north for the sun,
which had been his cell for most of the long anti-climax
of his career. An iron campaign bed, two portraits of his
wife, Marie-Louise of Austria, seven of his son, His Serene
Highness the Duke of Reichstadt, a mahogany table, writing-desk, a dressing-case by Biennais and, over the fireplace, a
watch which had belonged to Frederick the Great.

Then, helped by Marchand, he began his careful toilet,
washing and shaving in a silver washbasin from the Elysée
while Marchand held a mirror in front of him. Afterwards,
while Marchand massaged him with eau-de-cologne,
Napoleon thought about the women in his life and wondered
if, with his sickness dispelled, with freedom and power –
even token power – returned, his virility might return. He
thought about Josephine, for whom he had pined on the
battlefield and then divorced; he thought about Marie-Louise, his political wife who had borne him a son out of
passion; of the two, he had preferred Marie-Louise and

had confided this to Bertrand – "never a lie, never a debt". He recalled her words on their first night together: "Do it again." He thought, too, of the seven other women who had been able to boast that they had been bedded by the Emperor; in particular, he thought about a vivacious blonde named Madame Fourès, known to his troops in Egypt as Cleopatra. As Marchand's sensitive hands moved across his chest he thought of the conquests attributed to him on St Helena – the wives of both Montholon and Bertrand and sundry English misses. Well, it was only natural that his presence would create gossip and he had no intention of contradicting it.

After the massage the butcher Antornmarchi was admitted.

"And how is Your Majesty today?" the Corsican physician asked.

"You should know," Napoleon answered.

Antommarchi inclined his head. "Have you taken your tablets today, Sire?"

Napoleon shook his head. "I don't think they're necessary any longer. I shall have the symptoms swept away by the winds of freedom."

After the doctor had left, Napoleon occupied himself for a while with notes for his will; not the final draft yet. "... I die prematurely assassinated by the English oligarchy and their executioner: the English people will soon avenge me." Even if he didn't escape he would win the last battle: Lowe would be disgraced.

But what a pathetic victory over a man not worthy of being his opponent. He spun the globe in the corner of the room and took out his maps. This morning he re-fought the battle of Lodi a few days before he had entered Milan; he had been at the heart of the fighting at the bridge of the

Adda and it was there that he had felt the greatness that was his. Subsequently he had written: "It was only on the evening after Lodi that I realised I was a superior being and conceived the ambition of performing great things, which hitherto had filled my thoughts only as a fantastic dream."

Le Petit Caporal sighed. Performing such "great things" as gardening. He put on his floppy straw hat and slippers, slipped a handkerchief, lorgnette and gold watch into his pocket and walked into the garden where coolies were already at work laying flower beds and sunken paths. It was humid, with low cloud hiding the plateau from the sun. Soon it would rain.

Lutyens wandered into the garden and greeted Napoleon; at least, Napoleon thought, this languid young man was an improvement on some of the idiots who had been sent to spy on him. "Well," he said, "that's half of your day's work done. You've seen me once. Now you've only to get a glimpse of me in my bath and you've finished. Are you still using the spy-hole drilled in the wall by one of your predecessors?"

Lutyens smiled lazily. "I don't enjoy this work, sir. And I can assure you that I don't use a spy-hole – it would only give me a cold in the eye."

Pain suddenly stabbed Napoleon, making him wince.

"Are you all right, sir?"

"Yes, thank you. You may go now and report to the Nincompoop that the Emperor is working at planning another campaign – where to plant his petunias."

Lutyens bowed and wandered off.

Napoleon was joined by Bertrand, massaging his bald patch; he looked worried, but he always did. "Sire," he said, "I have some disturbing news."

Napoleon took off his straw hat, beloved of English cartoonists, and wiped his brow. "If it's about this man Blackstone in the cave I know all about it."

"Not just that, Sire." Bertrand told him about the incident two nights ago when Lieutenant Fairfax, who now faced a court-martial, had almost sunk a British warship. "His soldiers claim they saw a monster," Bertrand said. "And now the sea patrols at night are to be increased."

Napoleon pondered. "Saw a monster, did they? Very fanciful for the phlegmatic British. Had they been drinking? In my experience the British always have been. I should have fired Cognac at them instead of gunpowder at Waterloo."

"It seems they had been drinking, Your Majesty."

"Then let's hope all the patrols continue the habit. Perhaps French wine will prove to be our most powerful weapon."

"The increase in the patrols may delay us."

Napoleon put his hand to his mouth as though he were about to vomit. The spasm passed. "Then we shall have to accept the delay. Only, God knows, I can't wait much longer."

At 10.30 Napoleon went indoors for lunch – eggs beaten into milk soup and a little Roquefort cheese washed down with white wine diluted with water. Then, wearing a dressing-gown, he retired to the billiards room to make some alterations to his memoirs with Montholon. Cloud cocooned the house in silence; a few fat drops of rain fell in the dust outside.

They heard the sound of hoof-beats, oddly resonant in the thick atmosphere.

Napoleon looked up from a map. "Who is it, Montholon?"

Montholon went to the window and uttered an oath. "It can't be."

"Can't be what? Please explain yourself?"

"It's the English policeman, Blackstone."

Napoleon looked surprised. "But I thought…" He spread his hands wide, "…I told you that he was a man to watch."

Blackstone had wandered on the shores of unconsciousness for half an hour. He had been dimly aware of the sound of running water, several voices – one a woman's – the smell of the sea and rodent life. Then the dim, revolving lights had been extinguished as if someone had bandaged his eyes. There were hands around his legs and shoulders and a lot of arguing which seemed to be debating his fate. The woman's voice reached him more clearly than the men's. But whose voice was it? The girl from the Brown Bear in Bow Street who sometimes kept his bed warm at night?

Blackstone moaned and vomited. A man swore and they put him down on the slimy floor. The argument continued; Blackstone lost consciousness again. When he next came to in a limbo of disjointed impressions he was being carried. Up steps by the feel of it, with his bearers breathing heavily and swearing as they stumbled and scraped themselves against the wall.

At one stage they turned so that his head was at a lower level than his feet. The blood gathered in his head, thudding at the back where the blow had fallen; it spread into a broad ache before narrowing into a bullet of pain. Blackstone passed out again.

He dozed fitfully, surfacing from nightmares and plunging back into them. When he finally came to with any semblance of clarity his eyes were fixed on a brown mole.

"Mary," he muttered. Then: "Christ, what did we drink?"

"No," Louise Perkins said. "Not Mary. And you didn't drink anything in particular as far as I know."

Blackstone raised his head and focused. "You," he said.

"Yes, me. I won't ask you how you feel. Just lie back and take it easy. You've had a nasty crack on the back of the head."

Blackstone lay back. There was something nagging at his memory but he couldn't remember what it was. He dug into his memory but found only pain. "Any idea what happened?"

"You were found in the street outside. It could have been anyone – a soldier, sailor, footpad..."

"...beggarman, slave."

"They thought you were dead."

"Who were the optimists?"

"The landlord's daughter saw you from her window. She seems to have a soft spot for you, that one. You haven't one for her, have you, Blackie?"

Blackstone closed his eyes and groaned to avoid answering.

"Turn over," she told him.

He realised as he rolled on to his stomach that he was naked beneath the sheets. He wondered who had undressed him. He winced as she placed an ice-cold dressing on the wound. He turned, holding the dressing with one hand. "What are you doing here, anyway?"

"I thought we might resume our French lessons." Her violet eyes looked down at him crookedly.

"I shan't be much of a pupil this morning."

Louise Perkins regarded him thoughtfully. "No, I don't think you will," she said, as if she had been contemplating an elaboration of the usual grammar lesson.

"In fact I think I'd better try and get some sleep."

She sighed. "I suppose so. How do you think you'll be tomorrow?"

"Fit for anything, I shouldn't wonder." He pulled the sheets up to his neck. "How's your husband, by the way?"

"Much the same as usual. There's a terrible commotion on the island at the moment." She told him about Lieutenant Fairfax's moment of decision. "The Governor's trying to blame Randolph. You know, military security and all that. In fact he's trying to blame everyone. Fairfax is to be court-martialled and the way things are going I should think his soldiers will be shot at dawn. They say they saw a monster or something ridiculous."

Blackstone sat up abruptly, winced and lay down again. "A monster? Tell me about it."

Louise repeated the soldiers' brandy-smudged descriptions of the monster. It had now acquired a head and a body that emerged from the water in a series of loops. All that was missing was fiery breath.

"Odd," Blackstone murmured. "Very odd." He paused. "Did they really hit the *Racoon* amidships with one ball?"

"It seems like it."

"God," Blackstone exclaimed, "what marksmanship." He began to laugh but it hurt so he chose sleep instead.

He felt her lips brush him, then she was gone, her perfume lingering in his dreams.

The dreams were confused but they were not the lurching nightmares of a few hours earlier. They were dominated by the monster rising from the deep, water pouring from its great serpentine head. His breathing became more peaceful. He awoke at lunch-time, drank some broth and fell asleep again. The monster returned, more benign all the time, a friendly sort of creature that you could take for a walk down Piccadilly.

Then suddenly it changed shape and became a small, stout man with hair combed forward, one hand to his breast.

Blackstone awoke.

They faced each other across a table in the drawing-room beneath a portrait of Napoleon's son. The room was sparsely furnished, the chimney was blackened with smoke. The bookcases were packed with books and a couple lay open on the table – Molière and Racine. They drank coffee from blue cups painted with gold hieroglyphics and pictures of Egypt by Vivant Denon. Napoleon had Montholon with him; Blackstone was supported by Lutyens. Conversation was slow.

Blackstone took some snuff and said: "I want to know where you were at 1 a.m. the night before last."

Montholon translated and Napoleon spoke rapidly in French.

Lutyens said in a bored voice: "He says he's not accustomed to being questioned in this manner. He is the Emperor and if you continue to address him in this manner then the audience is concluded. He says you don't realise how honoured you are to be received. He wouldn't do the same for the Lackey."

Blackstone considered this; he couldn't blame Napoleon; nor did he want to humiliate him more than necessary. He wasn't even sure he wanted to stop him escaping; but he didn't want to be outsmarted.

"Tell him," Blackstone said, "that I'm sorry if my manner offends him. Tell him" – Blackstone grinned at Lutyens – "tell him that it's probably due to the translation. But tell him, nevertheless, that I have to ask these questions because there has been a report that he was seen in Jamestown at that time. Tell him I know it's ridiculous but I have to investigate. Explain that I have to make a report to Hudson Lowe" – Napoleon raised his eyebrows – "but try and give the impression that I have no sympathy with the Governor and, in fact, think he's a little touched." Blackstone touched his forehead.

While Lutyens translated, Blackstone examined the sallow features across the table. The blue-grey eyes, intelligent forehead, rounded chin, short neck; not particularly prepossessing and yet the power flowed across the table: the plump man with the sick eyes was in command. Blackstone sensed what had persuaded men blindly to follow this man; there weren't many people whose admiration Blackstone sought; this was one of them. For a moment he toyed with the idea of helping Napoleon to escape; this was the strength of Bonaparte and you had to be strong to resist him. Blackstone poured himself some coffee. If only there were a Wellington here instead of a Lowe.

Through Lutyens, Bonaparte asked: "Does Lowe know about this ludicrous report that I was seen in Jamestown?"

Blackstone shook his head. "And he probably never will. I was the man who thought I saw you. If I tell Lowe that he will double the security. I shall keep my counsel."

Bonaparte drummed podgy fingers on the table. "It has been calculated that I am watched by 125 sentries by day and by 72 at night. If he doubles that he will have to enlist his Corsican Rangers again."

"You will have to forgive me for asking this, Your Majesty, but I need to put my curiosity at rest. Were you at any time in Jamestown?"

"The furthest I've been in months is the Devil's Punch Bowl. Now, please do not pursue the point or you will be accusing me of being a liar. I shouldn't want that to happen because I like the stamp of you. Let's talk about happier things. I understand the British Army tried to sink a British man-o'-war the night before last. I wish you'd had more gunners like that at Trafalgar."

Blackstone ignored the niceties. "If you weren't in Jamestown then, sir, you must have a double."

Napoleon shrugged. "At 1 a.m. you say? Not the best time for identifying people. Had you by any chance taken a drink, Monsieur Blackstone? I know from experience that the British do tend to indulge occasionally."

"I wasn't drunk."

"But you could have been mistaken?"

Blackstone hesitated. "I could have been. At any rate I don't intend to communicate what I saw to the Governor."

Bonaparte looked at him quizzically and popped one of his liquorice sweets into his mouth. "Just where do your loyalties lie, Monsieur?"

"Here." Blackstone prodded his chest.

"An admirable place to keep them but they cannot remain caged all your life."

Outside the rain was falling harder, the opening musketry of the storm to come. The tick of the clock on the bookshelf sounded loud. Montholon broke the silence. "Tell me, Monsieur Blackstone, how strong is the feeling for the Emperor in England?"

"A lot of people believe that he should be accorded more dignity. They don't feel that it is … British for the victor to humiliate the vanquished." Blackstone, he thought, you've swallowed a dictionary.

Napoleon spoke. "And you, Monsieur Blackstone, what do you think?"

"I think I have to do my duty."

"Ah, England expects …."

"Do you intend to try and escape, Your Majesty?"

Even Napoleon was startled when the question was translated. "What do you expect me to answer? Yes, I intend to saddle a fast horse and ride to Rupert's Bay where there will be a cutter waiting for me? Unless you have anything more sensible to ask, Monsieur Blackstone, then I consider this interview at a close."

"But I have." Blackstone stood up. "I should like to re-live some of His Majesty's campaigns with him over his maps."

"Ah, a blunt man *and* a diplomat. An unusual combination. You are wasted here, Monsieur."

Blackstone bowed. "And so are you, Your Majesty."

Three hours later, as dusk was thickening, they finally straightened up from the maps. The garrison cannon announced sundown as if it had shot the sun out of the sky. The rain stopped and the insects started chirruping in the dripping foliage.

Blackstone took his leave, awed by the brain that had been functioning beside him. Let him go free, he thought, and he would raise another army and recapture Europe. Except for the sickness burning inside him.

Before leaving, Blackstone went with Lutyens to the quarters of Antommarchi, the physician. Antommarchi poured them wine. He had longish hair brushed forward, a slightly receding chin and a deeply meditative expression that could only mask a vacuum. As they stood around the fireplace Blackstone sipped his wine and asked: "Is Napoleon Bonaparte going to die?" Lutyens translated.

"That is for God to decide."

"God must have had a lot of dismal decisions to make with the knife in your hands."

"Please, I do not understand."

Lutyens translated again.

"You insult me, Monsieur?"

"Yes," Blackstone said.

"But why? I have no great claims to be a physician. I know my limitations."

"Then why did you take the job?"

"It was offered to me at a miserable salary. I accepted because the health of the Emperor was at stake."

"You accepted," Blackstone said, "because you knew you could never command a lot of blunt—"

"Blunt?" Lutyens queried.

"Money," Blackstone translated. "So you settled for glory. Napoleon Bonaparte's private physician. My God, man, you're made. I see that you've made the same diagnosis as the British physicians sacked by Sir Hudson Lowe. That didn't take a great deal of medical intelligence, did it?"

Lutyens interrupted. "But it did take a little courage. Anyone who's even suggested that Napoleon is really sick has got himself into trouble. Sir Hudson doesn't like his pet theory that Boney is malingering questioned."

Blackstone ignored him. "Ask him who's poisoning Napoleon."

Antommarchi looked surprised. "I beg your pardon?"

"Do you know anything about the medical symptoms of arsenic poisoning?"

"Of course."

"What are they?" Blackstone swallowed a mouthful of wine, wondering if it was poisoned.

"Faintness."

"Very good."

"Sickness."

"Excellent."

"Vomiting." There was a note of hesitancy in the Corsican's voice.

"Superb deduction, Antommarchi. We could do with you at Bow Street."

"I am sorry?"

Lutyens yawned. "Really, Blackie, you're not God's gift to an interpreter. Besides," he added, "I think we should adjourn to my rooms and have some brandy."

"Napoleon's right about you British," Blackstone said, "you're all lushy."

"What do you want me to ask him?"

"More symptoms of arsenic poisoning, please."

Antommarchi pondered and drank some wine.

"I don't think he knows any more," Lutyens said. "He's only ever dealt with the final symptom."

"Ask him about the stomach. Are there any distinguishing marks on the stomach?"

"On the belly, you mean?"

"If you wish."

Lutyens asked the Corsican and told Blackstone: "He thinks there might be."

"Very enlightening. Ask him if he's ever seen any marks like ... like rain-drops on Napoleon's stom ... belly."

Lutyens asked Antommarchi, who shook his head, looking at Blackstone as if he were crazy.

Blackstone said to Lutyens: "The trouble, of course, is that the symptoms are much the same as those of cholera."

"But you don't think Boney's got cholera? He's lasting too long."

"I don't know what to think."

"He'd be dead if he'd had cholera all this time."

"Ask him about Cipriani. What does he think he died of?"

The Corsican shook his head helplessly.

"He doesn't know," Lutyens said.

"Thank you, I gathered that."

"Do you think he was poisoned?" Lutyens asked.

"Most people on the island seem to think so. Odd, isn't it, that he was present at the campaign when Lowe was humiliated. Odd, isn't it, that Lowe is being humiliated right now and Napoleon is suffering from symptoms that could be attributed to poisoning."

Lutyens looked uncharacteristically thoughtful. "Very odd," he agreed. "Now, have you any other questions to ask the butcher? If not let's adjourn and sup a little brandy. I never really know about this business about seeing Boney twice a day. Surely if I see him having breakfast, close my eyes and open them again that's enough?"

"I congratulate you," Blackstone said, "on your devotion to duty."

"I'm not a snooper."

"Nor me."

"Then let's pack it in and go and have a drink."

Antommarchi pointed at Blackstone's face and spoke quickly.

"What's he saying?"

"He says you're suffering from a head wound and you shouldn't be drinking."

Blackstone said: "That confirms my opinion of his medical talents. Let's go and have a drink."

Three hours later Blackstone rode the five miles back to Jamestown. The stars swam above him and he had forgotten about the symptoms of arsenic poisoning, cholera and hepatitis. But in the morning, he thought, there would be multiple symptoms of the effects of a blow on the head compounded by excessive intake of alcohol.

CHAPTER TEN

Watching the rats outside the officers' mess, Blackstone thought of London's rats, leaner and quicker than the rats that plagued St Helena (one was said to have nested in Napoleon's hat), darting along the banks of the streams – Tyborne, Hole Borne, the Fleet, West Borne. Beneath London's streets there was another twilight world of tunnels and sewers and secret passages; one day he would investigate the city beneath the city and write a book about it. If he ever got away from St Helena.

The mess was a gloomy, wooden place at Deadwood and everything in it was dead. Glass-eyed trophies on the walls, spiked guns, dried flowers, the mess steward. Blackstone yawned and sipped his malt whisky. Perkins was deep in a sheaf of papers, reading them like a professor on the brink of a discovery; Lutyens was asleep, mouth wide open in his imperturbable face. Tonight there was to be a ball at Deadwood and Blackstone supposed he would have to attend. There were still a few dignitaries he hadn't met; in particular Claude Marin Henri, Marquis de Montchenu, known to the British as Old Munch Enough, commissioner of the King of France. Originally, under the Convention signed in Paris on 2 August 1815, commissioners had been appointed for Russia, Austria and France; only Munch Enough remained. He was elderly, pompous and amorous;

yet another nincompoop, Blackstone thought; St Helena seemed to attract them as if buffoonery were imported as a buffer to Napoleon's greatness.

Blackstone stretched himself. In the corner, in a leather easy chair, a colonel with fat thighs snored. Thank God for the rats, Blackstone thought, at least they were alive. He ordered another whisky from the steward, who briefly came to life.

Perkins looked up from his papers. "Military security seems sound enough," he pronounced.

"Except when the army tries to sink British ships," Blackstone said.

"They were drunk."

"Hardly the basis for sound security."

"But you can't stop them drinking," Perkins said, "or they'd mutiny."

"And you say security's sound?"

Perkins nodded his handsome head. "Frigates anchored at every possible landing place. Two brigs – more now – circling the island day and night. A shot fired as soon as a strange ship is sighted and a reward of a piastre for the first sighting.... I hear an American ship which tried to enter the harbour in bad weather was threatened that she would be fired on if she didn't remove herself. Passwords, a curfew on the centre of the island, watch-outs and look-outs and sentries at every corner. I ask you, what chance has Bonaparte of getting away?"

"I don't know," said Blackstone, gazing at the man he had agreed to fight a duel with on their return to London, "but I have a feeling something's up."

"A pox on your ideas," Perkins said. He waved one glittering hand angrily, picked up a pair of field glasses and gazed in the direction of Alarm House. "Anyway, he's still there at the moment."

The British had installed a system of flags at Alarm House indicating Bonaparte's movements:

Everything under control
General Bonaparte is not well
General Bonaparte is out beyond the cordon of sentries but under observation
General Bonaparte is out, but inside the cordon
General Bonaparte has been out beyond the cordon longer than usual and is not properly attended
General Bonaparte has vanished

The last message, a blue flag, fluttered in Sir Hudson Lowe's nightmares.

"Then you can relax," Blackstone told Perkins.

"You don't seem too concerned about your responsibility."

"In the end it must be military security that prevails."

Perkins considered this gloomily. "Do you really think there's any plot? I mean it is your responsibility to tell me if you've heard anything."

"Nothing definite. Just my sixth sense."

Blackstone hadn't told Perkins about the cave. In any case, when he pulled back the table in the parlour that morning it had been blocked with bricks. He had decided to keep Montholon, the most dangerous man at Longwood, under surveillance, still not sure whether he wanted to foil an escape.

In the corner the colonel fought and won an old battle, awoke with a snort of triumph, glared around and went back to sleep. The rats twitched their whiskers, Perkins returned to his papers, Lutyens closed his mouth. Thus the conference on the island's security continued.

Idly Blackstone sorted through a pile of newspapers, all several months old. The accession of Prinny to the throne, the first iron steamship, a review of Keats's "Hyperion", some letters about the plight of Napoleon.

He picked up a copy of *The Times,* its pages yellowing and covered with circles from slopping cups and glasses. His attention was caught by an article about attempts to build a practicable vessel capable of manoeuvring underwater. Herodotus, Aristotle and Pliny the Elder had apparently discussed the construction of diving bells in a thirteenth-century manuscript called *La Vraie Histoire d' Alexandre* and Alexander the Great had been lowered in a glass barrel to the sea-bed.

Blackstone yawned, glanced around at the somnolent scene and read on.

"Well," Perkins said, gathering up his papers, "time to be off."

"I'll join you later."

"What are you reading so avidly?"

"The racing results," Blackstone told him.

Perkins made a noise implying that he expected nothing more and departed.

Lutyens smacked his lips in his sleep.

The colonel groaned at some ancient defeat.

Blackstone read on.

In 1800 an American, Robert Fulton, designed an underwater ship named *Nautilus,* made from wood covered with iron plates. It had a sail, hand-driven screw propeller, tower and a porthole.

Blackstone stopped with one finger on the column of print. His finger shook. *Fulton had built an underwater vessel for Napoleon!* But the project had been abandoned because, at two knots, it was too slow.

Blackstone stared across the plateau to the open sea where the "monster" had surfaced. Had the project been resurrected? He put down *The Times*. He felt his excitement must disturb the somnolence. But what to do? It was surely an act of inhumanity to prevent a bid by a once-great man to end his days with some vestige of dignity. And yet. ... Blackstone took his baton from his pocket and stared at the crown. The crown was his loyalty irrespective of the monarch it represented, irrespective of that monarch's second-rate representative on St Helena.

Blackstone stood up. He had to escape the torpor around him. He left Lutyens with his mouth opening again, the colonel resting between battles; he prodded the steward with his baton to see if sawdust spilled out and left the mess. Outside he mounted his horse and galloped away across the plain towards the sea.

Cloud hung like a plate over the centre of the island but soon he was outside its shadow, with the sun beating down, the sky deep and blue, the sea a sparkling triangle through a valley in the mountains. He slowed to a canter, waving his baton at a military patrol. What should he do?

Blackstone breathed deeply of the scents of blossom and sea, shook his head and turned the horse towards Jamestown, having made the indecisive decision to postpone making any move until the garrison ball at which Sir Hudson Lowe would be present.

The bad news was brought to Napoleon after mass in the dining-room which did duty as a chapel. It had been an indifferent day – weren't they all? – with a drive beside the Devil's Punch Bowl, an attack of vertigo in the garden beside the sunken pools, dinner with his favourite dessert, banana fritters marinated in rum. Now he was reading *Paul et Virginie* and trying to ignore the attack of nausea.

Bertrand was the bearer of the news; bad news seemed to be his mission in life. He was massaging the bald spot; perhaps, Napoleon thought, over the years he had rubbed the hair away.

"Well?" Napoleon put the book down. "What is it this time?"

Bertrand confirmed the expression on his face. There had been a set-back. When Lieutenant Fairfax fired his cannon, the underwater vessel had submerged too hastily.

Napoleon clenched his dimpled fists. Where was the vessel now? he asked. The worsening expression on Bertrand's face told him. Napoleon pointed downwards with his thumb. "Down there?"

The Grand Marshal nodded.

"And the crew?"

Bertrand pointed downwards with his thumb.

"Poor devils," Napoleon murmured. "What a death. I have seen some terrible deaths on the battlefield but none as bad as that." He paused, imagining the men in the ship struggling to escape, water pouring in through an insecure door; the hull cracking open like an eggshell.

"They died for a good cause," Bertrand said.

"Did they?" Napoleon gazed through the window of his prison. "Did they, Bertrand? Did they die for a good cause or did they die to satisfy the vanity of a sick man who would have done well to die at Waterloo?"

Bertrand said stiffly: "The greatest man France has ever known must not be allowed to end his days as the prisoner of a grubby English warder. He must have the last victory."

"However puny that victory?"

"However small, Sire. You must beat the British, the shop-keepers, in the end."

"I suppose so." Napoleon walked to the window and gazed at the stars, the panoply on the eve of so many glorious battles. "How long now, Bertrand?"

"Obviously there will be a delay."

"I asked how long."

"At least three months," Bertrand said quietly.

"God!" The sweat on his body ran cold and he thought he might faint. He sat down. "Another three months of this? Another three months fighting a war of attrition more worthy of a schoolboy?"

"We must continue as before, Sire. As if we were determined to sit it out, not yielding until. ..."

"I die?"

"Until the end, Your Majesty." Bertrand peered at Napoleon. "Are you ill? Shall I send for Antommarchi?"

"No," Napoleon said, "I am not a corpse yet."

Blackstone was dancing with Lady Lowe. The dance gave him little pleasure. She was trying unsuccessfully to combine coquetry with the dignity of her station. Blackstone wasn't sure whether she was flirtatious on her own behalf or on account of her unmarried daughters, the eldest having been married to Alexander Antonovitch Ramsay de Balmain, the Russian commissioner at St Helena who had taken his bride to Russia. Blackstone thought it doubtful that she fancied a Bow Street Runner in the family; it was more likely that she wanted to spite her husband.

"A few hearts have fluttered since your arrival in our little community," Lady Lowe said as they swirled round the improvised ballroom. "You seem to have a way with the ladies." Her breath smelled of alcohol and there was a high colour to her cheeks.

"You're very kind," Blackstone said. He wished someone would fire a warning cannon or something; he was as fond of dancing as he was of linguistics.

"You must come to another of our dinner parties. Smaller and more select than the last one."

"Does the invitation come from your husband?"

Her attitude changed infinitesimally. "I am perfectly entitled to invite whomsoever I please to dinner. I shall ask Gorrequer to attend to it."

"I shall be honoured," Blackstone lied.

They skated round a corner polished with French chalk and Blackstone spotted the pinched, sandy face of the Governor staring at them with displeasure.

"This wasn't your husband's dance by any chance?" he asked hopefully. Lady Lowe had a reputation for being an accomplished hostess and a gossip with a talent for embarrassing Sir Hudson with ill-timed actions.

Lady Lowe hiccuped softly. "I told him that I wanted to dance with the Bow Street Runner."

"Bow Street Dancer." Blackstone smiled wanly.

The dance finished with a frothy swirl of dresses, kissing of hands and creaking of joints. The ladies were escorted back to their places by the officers in their peacock uniforms.

Blackstone approached Sir Hudson Lowe. He knew that he had to discard sentimentality and tell the Governor what he suspected about underwater escape plans for Napoleon. It was part of the new discipline he had learned and he detested it. Even now he prayed for a way out; a justification for keeping his theories to himself.

Sir Hudson left the knot of officers surrounding him. "Well?"

"Could I have a few words with you, sir?"

"I thought you preferred to confide in General Bonaparte."

"I have my duty to do."

"In fact I'm surprised to find you here. I should have thought the parlour of the tavern you inhabit was much more your mark. They tell me the serving wenches there are very comely. However, what is it you wanted to tell me?"

Blackstone stared at him for a moment. "Nothing," he said. "Nothing at all, Your Excellency."

PART TWO

CHAPTER ONE

The brig with the "monster" hatching in its womb made good speed in the January of 1821 with a stiff breeze behind her and no storms forcing her to linger in safe anchorage. As she sailed south, the coast of Africa smudging the horizon, a gang of carpenters worked feverishly on the embryo of the underwater vessel conceived on dry land. It was, thought the captain of the brig, standing on the bridge, a very noisy gestation.

He had been told it was a matter of life and death to reach St Helena as soon as possible. For each day out of the normal run to Jamestown he was to receive a bonus of £50 on top of the already generous payment. The skipper, who had the looks and habits of a pirate, made very good time indeed, even brushing aside a slaver offering finely-muscled Negroes at bargain prices.

Down below the clatter continued.

The ship within the ship was about sixty feet long, shaped like a cigar with four oars protruding from apertures made water-tight with big leather washers, and a hand-operated propeller. The framework was iron with a wooden hull; on top was an observation tower through which a member of the crew could scan the waves for the enemy while the rest of the structure was underwater. The ship submerged and surfaced with water ballast; at least that was the theory;

privately, the skipper thought that it would only go one way and that wasn't upwards. It was designed for a crew of five and one passenger – one short, plumpish passenger. The skipper of the brig admired the courage of the man who was going to pilot the underwater craft; he, too, was going to be paid handsomely but what, the skipper of the brig reasoned, was the use of a fortune at the bottom of the South Atlantic?

They were close to the Canaries when they saw the whirlwind moving across the sea. The skipper stared in its direction, keeping his hand over the end of his telescope. The mate, a one-eyed Frenchman who had fought at Trafalgar, pointed at the shadow spinning as innocently as a top. "I don't like the look of it, sir," he said.

"Don't like the look of what?"

"That." Pointing at the black spinning-top.

"I see no whirlwind," said the skipper.

The mate refrained from pointing out that he hadn't mentioned a whirlwind. The last member of the crew who had disagreed with the skipper was in chains down below.

The captain gave the order to get up more sail. The brig gathered a little speed but, apart from the phenomenon on the horizon, the wind that thrust them so briskly past the coast of Europe had blown itself out. The calm before the storm, the mate thought miserably. Fifty pounds a day, thought the skipper, staring hard at the coast of Africa.

Fish were popping excitedly and, from the bridge, they could see the fins of half a dozen sharks making for shelter. But there was a lot of ocean around and it would surely be against all the odds, reasoned the skipper, if the whirlwind hit them. If it did then the brig would become an underwater vessel and brigs weren't designed to resurface.

They could see the core of the whirlwind now, like a stick surrounded by a swarm of gnats. A toy-thing of the ocean which could topple coastal towns in its path like play-bricks.

Above the bridge the sails were limp. Below, the work went on, the carpenters singing as if they were rowing in the galley. The man in chains passed the time devising ways in which the skipper could be used as ballast for the under-water ship.

The whirlwind, about three miles away, made as if to pass, bowling across the ocean towards the Americas. The skipper grinned, humming "Fifty pounds a day, Fifty pounds a day" to the accompaniment of the carpenters; the mate complimented him on his seamanship.

Then, as if it had smelled this rash optimism, the whirlwind altered course. It came in pursuit like a hunt after one fox in an open field. Even the winds, the skipper thought, are in the employ of the British. Three miles, still closing.

Ahead lay the harbour of Santa Cruz, lazing in the sun. What the hell was the use of £50 a day to a drowned man? You couldn't pay off the eels with bank notes. The skipper gave orders to sail in the direction of the port. There was just a chance that, if they were hit by the outer currents of the whirlwind, they would be bowled towards the island; if they were sucked into the centre then they were doomed.

Lazily, the brig turned towards the island.

The avenging whirlwind loomed closer so that the crew of the brig could distinguish its physique, its veins, its skirts of sea-water sucked up from the ocean. The carpenters stopped singing and came on deck. A few prayed, but the majority stared helplessly at the primeval wrath chasing them, each aware of his awesome unimportance in the scheme of things.

It was about a mile away now, filling the sky, fish and weed swirling around the dark pillar of the axis. The skipper gave the order to break the chains of the insubordinate below. He spread wide his arms. "Why?" he asked the heavens. "The whole ocean. Why us?"

The mate ventured: "Shouldn't we take to the boats?"

"Anyone who wants to make quite sure of drowning is welcome to do so. Tell them that."

No one moved.

It was almost on top of them now. They could feel its cold breath; it smelled like wet earth after rain. They prayed, repented, reminded God of all the good deeds they had committed.

Suddenly the whirlwind veered away once more as if it had spotted a sleeker, fatter prey. The hem of its skirts caught the brig and shovelled it forward on a great wave. The brig hurtled forward, losing a couple of guns and a couple of men overboard, and stormed the harbour, smashing into the quayside. One of its two masts cracked and fell with a slow, easy motion on to the deck.

"Where are they for God's sake?" Montholon's noble face was anguished.

Bertrand massaged his scalp. "Perhaps the British Navy intercepted them."

"Why should they do that?"

"I don't know. It could have happened." The Grand Marshal's face was creased with worry. "A storm perhaps?"

Montholon smote the table where they were dining with his fist. "If they don't come soon then it will be too late."

Since the new year the condition of the patient at Longwood House had deteriorated dramatically. His plump cheeks had caved in and he could only stomach soup, arrow-root and jelly.

On 17 March he went for a ride in his carriage, vomited and took to his bed. Bed, he told Marchand, was the most comfortable throne in the world and the only one he sought.

On 22 March Francesco Antommarchi, muttering about gastric fever, administered two tartaric emetics. His patient fell to the ground in agony. There was consternation at Longwood that the Corsican butcher might have dealt a mortal blow and would soon be carrying out the work he knew best – attending to a cadaver.

Sir Hudson Lowe reacted dramatically to the confinement. Lutyens hadn't seen Napoleon for several days and Lowe insisted that the patient show himself. If he didn't then the door to his bedroom would be forced. Bertrand and Montholon decided to call in a British doctor to reassure Lowe and, on 1 April, a forty-nine-year-old Scot, Dr Archibald Arnott of the 20th Regiment, was called in.

Arnott, recalling the fate of his predecessors who had taken Napoleon's complaints seriously, told Lowe that Napoleon's condition was mental, that he was suffering from hypochondria. In his diary Major Gideon Gorrequer recorded that Lowe interpreted Napoleon's condition as "the reflection of his impolite conduct here and his behaviour to him". Lowe, wrote Gorrequer, had said: "If a person was to go in there and make a great clamour it would be the most likely thing to revive him. Depend on it."

The patient at Longwood said: "I'm not afraid of dying, the only thing I'm afraid of is that the English will keep my body and put it in Westminster Abbey."

Every day reports from look-outs reached Longwood House through the French spy network of slaves, servants and British soldiers, particularly men of the 20th Regiment who respected Napoleon more than Lowe. Every day the patient's condition deteriorated until even Archibald Arnott had to agree that Napoleon was physically ill. In consultation with Antommarchi he prescribed potions to open the bowels and quinine to ease the fever. The patient responded with traces of blood in his vomit.

On 13 April he began to make his last will, which he had toyed with before. He said he wanted to die in the apostolic Roman religion and wanted his ashes taken to the banks of the Seine "in the midst of the French people whom I have loved so well"

To Montholon he left 2 million francs; to Bertrand 500,000; to Marchand, his valet, 400,000.

"Soon," Montholon said, "very soon it will be too late. All that planning. ... Surely God can't be so cruel."

"God moves in a mysterious way," Bertrand quoted.

A Chinese coolie, Number Nine, sidled into the room. The generals looked at him expectantly. "Any news?"

Number Nine shook his head sadly. The way things were going all sources of gold pieces would soon dry up.

The irony was that the underwater vessel named the *Shark* was finished before the brig was repaired. It lay snug and complete in the womb of the mother ship while the carpenters tackled the brig's fractured hull and erected a new mast. The skipper abandoned all hope of his bounty and drank in surly isolation in the town's bars.

After they had languished in the sunshine for two weeks it was decided to make a trial run with the *Shark*. She was rowed out to sea with a single sail and curious observers on the harbourside were told that she was an experimental fishing boat designed by an eccentric nobleman.

The sky was cloudless and the blue water, in which shoals of tiny fish were suspended, looked very deep. The *Shark*'s captain and his crew of four stood on the deck beside the squat tower, breathing the salt air, watching the gulls wheeling in the sky. The reality to which avarice had brought them was the cold hand of imminent death.

"What happens if we don't go through with it?" one of the crew asked.

"They'll shoot us," the captain said. He was a man of about fifty with pale blue eyes, a bullet scar surrounded by puckered skin on one cheek and a mottled complexion; it was the face of an adventurer tempered by middle-age and the knowledge that he had to make a pile for his old age in one last fling.

Another member of the crew said: "I'm calling it off." He pointed into the depths, beyond the bars of sunlight and the shivering fish, down into the unfathomable shadows of the ocean. "I don't want the sharks to get me. I don't want my lungs filled with water. We were mad to ever consider it."

The sun beat down on them; the air was fresh and sweet.

The third member of the crew said: "What did Napoleon ever do for us?" He shivered despite the heat.

The fourth member said: "If we were intended to go underwater we would have been given gills. If we were intended to fly we would have been given wings. I don't want to do either, let's get back to the shore."

"And be shot?" the captain asked, fingering the scar on his cheek.

"Better be shot than drowned," the first man said. "At least we could make a fight of it."

The captain said: "If we betrayed Napoleon we would be pursued to the ends of the earth. Besides," he said, "aren't we forgetting the money we're getting? A fortune for each of us." Ten times as much for me, he thought. "And for a small risk. This isn't the first ship built to go underwater. They're as safe as houses. If you notice a leak when you're just below the surface come up again and abandon the whole idea. Think of the money, lads," he said, his voice thick with greed, "just think of the swag."

The second man said: "To hell with the money. I'm calling it off. I want to stay alive."

A flying fish took to the air and dived into the sea again.

"You see," the skipper said, "that was meant for the water but it takes to the air."

"Good luck to it," the crewman muttered. "I'm not going down there to meet the sharks. I'll risk a bullet." He turned to the other three. "What about it, lads? Do you want to be buried in Davy Jones' Locker?"

The skipper said: "You will be if the sharks don't get you first." He took a double-barrelled flint-lock from his pocket and shot the seaman through the chest. The seaman clutched at his chest, looked down at the blood pouring from between his hands, stepped back into the sea. He floated for a few moments, pleading with the rest of the crew to pull him back, his blood making red lacework among the bars of sunlight. A hundred yards away a black fin surfaced, then another. The water around the wounded man became agitated. The two sharks circled him twice then homed in, taking his legs. His face disappeared and the water went on boiling for five minutes. Then it began to grow calm again as the two black triangles headed out to sea.

"Well?" asked the captain, "what about it, lads?" He held a pistol in each hand now.

"You cold-blooded bastard," one of the crew said.

"Are you going under or not?"

They opened the hatch and climbed down the ladder, the captain bringing up the rearguard. He battened down the hatch and seated himself at the controls of the screw propeller. "I suggest, lads," he said, "that you forget what happened up there. An accident at sea, that's what it was. We're all in this together so we'll sink or swim together. And maybe we'll become rich together. Are you going to cooperate?"

They consulted and finally agreed.

"Right, well we're only making sure that she goes down and comes up all right. We're not concerned with speed so, as one of our oarsmen is missing, we'll just have two of you rowing. When we're under I'll try out this contraption," he said, indicating the controls of the propeller.

There were two portholes and, on either side of the cabin, six leather containers like elephantine bottles. "Right," said the captain, "two of you start letting the water in, one to each container. I'll light the lantern."

Gingerly, with shaking hands, they unscrewed the taps connecting the leather bags to the sea. Water whooshed in, two of the bags expanded like balloons. The *Shark* lurched downwards; daylight dimmed outside the portholes; they looked out into green water.

"Shut them off," the captain shouted. The two men grappled with the taps; the water stopped flowing in. Daylight still entered the cabin from the observation porthole in the tower. The captain took a couple of steps up the ladder and peered through it; his eyes were level with the sea and every ripple looked like a tidal wave. "Man the oars," he said.

They pulled strongly, turning the clumsy, broad-bladed oars in the water-tight row-locks so that they could manipulate them back with the least water resistance. In the tower the captain saw the water slide past. "We're moving," he shouted. "It works."

He returned to the controls and began to turn the heavy wheel. The *Shark* accelerated. "Now," he said, "we must try and submerge completely. No use trying to get through the British blockade with the tower sticking above the water."

The crew looked apprehensive. "Aren't we deep enough for a maiden voyage?" one of them asked.

"We're not." The captain picked up his pistol and waved the barrel at the leather bags. "Fill another couple."

The men were sweating cold, underwater sweat. The bags filled up and the daylight entering through the tower turned to dusk, to night. They were in a cave lit by a single candle-lantern.

One of them moaned with fear. The captain stopped working the propeller; the silence was thick.

The captain said: "Start pumping the air, one of you. That will be the job for our passenger if we ever get there."

The air entered by a hollow mast which could be raised above the tower and was circulated by a fan. As the fan began to whirl they smelled salt air and relaxed a little.

The captain grinned. He climbed the steps and looked through the porthole; the water was light green; he saw an object floating just above eye-level and tried to make out what it was. After a few seconds he identified it: it was the savaged remnants of a human hand.

He climbed down again. He said: "Right, lads, it works. We're on to a fortune. We could go deeper – in fact we'll have to at St Helena – but we won't bother now. One more trial run and we're ready. The other *Shark*" – conscious that he was making a mistake by referring to its loss – "went down because they had two trials. We know enough from what they learned to make it under the British ships in one run."

"Why did you have to bring that up?" One of the oars-men stood up, fear cutting his words to shreds. "Let's get back to the surface for Christ's sake."

"All right, two of you on to the water containers."

They fixed a powerful iron clamp operated on a screw round the first bag. They opened the taps and screwed the jaws of the clamp around the leather. The bag emptied, the *Shark* tilted, infinitesimally, the darkness outside lightened. They did the same to the other three and they were on the surface again with sunlight, life-light, pouring through the portholes. The captain opened the hatch and they clambered on to the deck.

They breathed in great, shuddering gulps.

Finally one of them grinned and said: "Nothing to it. In a few months we'll all be rich men."

They all laughed, drunk with fresh air.

The captain said: "Boney, here we come."

On 27 April, as the brig approached the gauntlet of British ships around St Helena, the sick man at Longwood House vomited a liquid resembling coffee grounds. He complained of being bitterly cold and his feet were warmed with hot towels. He said he couldn't breathe in his small room and he was moved into the drawing-room.

By the beginning of May, with time running out like a fast tide, the stage was set for the escape.

CHAPTER TWO

Blackstone kept his body fit by riding and swimming; but, as the months dawdled past, he could feel his brain growing soggy with routine and boredom. Since he had felt the exhilaration of the chase of human quarry across Britain and Europe, he could no longer stay put for any length of time. And he had been in St Helena a long, long time.

Since Hudson Lowe's snub he had bothered himself little with the possibility of Napoleon escaping; in fact he had begun to hope that *Le Petit Caporal* would make a getaway; whenever his conscience stirred he assuaged it with the belief that escape was impossible for a man in Napoleon's state of health.

For a while he occupied himself investigating the possibility that Napoleon was being poisoned. The Irish physician, Dr Barry O'Meara, dismissed by Hudson Lowe because he had diagnosed that Napoleon was seriously ill, had already implied that Lowe had asked him to administer poison. But Blackstone got nowhere; he needed unbiased medical opinion and there wasn't any on the island. It seemed to Blackstone quite feasible that Antommarchi was in the pay of Lowe and was administering the poison; he warned the French through Lutyens but no action was taken.

So Blackstone went for his daily ride in the mists of the plateau, roamed the tropic finery of the farmlands, bathed from the rocks and, two or three times a week, made love to Lucinda Darnell. But even this was becoming monotonous; and when making love to a girl like Lucinda became monotonous there was something horribly wrong. And it was complicated by Louise Perkins.

Louise Perkins was a girl unaccustomed to rejection. She herself had rejected many a military suitor with jingling medals and clashing spurs; and had enjoyed the dismissal, the feeling of power over men that it gave her. But to be rejected herself was unthinkable. She knew her body was magnificent, she knew the set of her violet eyes was an attribute which aroused men's curiosity. Why then was Edmund Blackstone so impervious to her?

After his accident she nursed him patiently, even though he was galloping around the island within two days. She arrived in the morning, stroking his brow and brushing his face with her bosom, massaging the powerful muscles at the base of his neck and allowing her fingers to stray down his chest towards his hard flat belly; but somehow it always ended there; he treated her as a nurse. It was humiliating.

She invited him to dinner despite the fact that he was due to fight a duel with her husband. She danced with him most of the evening at a ball at Plantation House which Blackstone attended reluctantly; she contrived meetings on horseback on the plateau; she caught him bathing in the nude and was astonished and excited when he walked past her, still naked, dried himself and dressed as if he were changing after polo. It angered her to think that he was so casual about dressing and so obstinate about undressing.

For his part, Blackstone was as wary of Louise Perkins as ever. For one thing he didn't make a habit of making love to other men's wives; for a second he knew the extent of Lucinda Darnell's jealousy; for a third he sensed that

Louise was a calculating and dangerous woman. She was, he suspected, the sort of woman who got you into bed and then hollered that she had been raped.

So, whenever violet-eyed danger threatened, Blackstone took evasive action, usually to the parlour of the Good Neighbour where he was beginning to drink too much. He was often joined there by Lutyens, who was equally bored with his duties as tame watchdog at Longwood. On the night of 16 April 1821 they sat drinking dog's noses, introduced to the island by Blackstone, and bemoaning their plight.

Lutyens took a long pull at his drink, shuddered and said: "I can't take it much longer." He had accepted a copy of *The Life of Marlborough* presented by Napoleon to the 20th Regiment and had been reproved by his commanding officer, Major Edward Jackson.

"Buy yourself out," Blackstone advised, "and join the Bow Street Runners."

"Perhaps I will."

Blackstone gazed muzzily at his friend. "Not you, you're not villainous enough."

"Not as villainous as you, perhaps, but bad enough."

"How's Boney?" Blackstone asked.

"Pretty bad. He's having an altar put up in one of the rooms so that Vignali the priest can administer extreme unction there. Says he was born a Catholic and wants to fulfil the duties it imposes and receive the help it affords."

"Poor devil," Blackstone said. "I wish there was something we could do."

Lutyens, dressed like an East India Company clerk because the Good Neighbour wasn't the place for officers, said: "It's getting worse there every day with Lowe in a panic about Boney's condition. We've got another batch of soldiers dressed as footmen with orders to report every movement back to Plantation House. And, of course, we've got the coolies." He nodded meaningfully at Blackstone. "But you know all about the coolies, eh, Blackie?"

"You mean Number Nine?" Blackstone never gave anyone the impression that they had caught him out. "He brings me the odd scrap of gossip. Nothing very important. What he can't find out he makes up."

According to Number Nine, Blackstone had been attacked by the dumb Negro because it was presumed he would break up the gang selling wines and spirits stolen from the French cellars. What other purpose could his presence serve, they had reasoned, on an island handcuffed by military security? Number Nine told Blackstone that his information came from a slave called Hannibal who worked closely with a Chinaman known as Number Thirteen. Did Blackstone want to interview them? Blackstone spoke to Hannibal and formed the opinion that the Negro was working with Number Nine: a minor operation to get a few more gold pieces out of him. Why, he asked Hannibal, had it been necessary to garrot the dumb Negro? Hannibal had been vague, presumably not wanting to be an accomplice to murder. Blackstone gave him a couple of sovereigns to help him save his passage to England.

Lutyens and Blackstone were joined by Jack Darnell who sat down, hooked arm swinging like a pendulum off the arm of the chair. Blackstone looked at his bearded face speculatively. He and Darnell both knew that they were sitting over the mouth of a secret tunnel. I should have done more about that, he thought, before the rot set in. But what was the point? Even if Napoleon had found some way of reaching the cellars of the tavern it didn't matter any longer: Napoleon was bed-ridden, a dying man. And Blackstone, who still felt guilty about Darnell's wooden arm, had no wish to delve into his smuggling activities.

Darnell ordered another round of dog's noses, massaged his wooden arm which, he said, sometimes pained him as if it were flesh and bone, and told them he had heard that Napoleon was about to ask for extreme unction.

"When did you hear that?" Blackstone asked. "Two minutes ago I'll wager, with those great flapping ears of yours."

"Never thought I'd see you developing into a lushington," Darnell said, ignoring the remark. "You were never a great one for the mecks in Devon. You liked a drink, I'll grant you that, but never on this scale."

"Set 'em up again, landlord," Lutyens said.

"You kanurd as well?" Darnell sighed. "An officer and a gentleman and a thief catcher both drunk. It pains me to take your blunt."

Blackstone's boredom had given way to genial intoxication. "I remember we sank a few together in the Castle at Dartmouth, Jack."

"Aye," Darnell said, filling his stocky pipe. "I was sensible in those days. I hadn't decided to trust you."

For a moment Blackstone worried. Dartmouth had alerted some instinct. There was a message there for him. What the hell could it be? He shook his head and drowned the worry with another dog's nose. Across the parlour Lucinda Darnell smiled at him and he winked back. I'm going soft, he thought; decadent; but at that moment, with some sailors singing a shanty and the rain tapping at the windows and the company pleasant and another drink in front of him, it didn't seem to matter.

Darnell said: "Ever think of getting married, Blackie?"

Blackstone sobered up a little. "I suppose every man does at some time or another," he ventured.

"You could do worse," Darnell said, watching him over the rim of his glass.

"Worse than what?"

"You know what, Blackie. I knows you've been dabbing it up with Lucy. I might have got only one arm but I've got two eyes. And ears," he added.

"You've dabbed it up with a few in your time, culley."

"I'll grant you that. And never got nobbled neither. Except, of course, by Lucy's mother."

Lutyens looked faintly embarrassed. "I think I ought to get back to my duties. Not that it matters too much these days with Archibald Arnott seeing Boney all the time." He made no move to leave. Darnell patted the table with his hook. "Don't you bother yourself, my dear. Blackie and I understand each other."

"What dowry are you offering?" Blackstone asked.

Darnell shrugged. "A tavern on St Helena?"

"Jesting again," Blackstone replied. "If you want to get rid of me, Jack, that's the way to go about it."

Lutyens said in a slurred voice: "I think I feel like a woman."

Blackstone said: "You might feel like one, my covey, but are you up to one?"

"I should call you for that remark."

"For God's sake don't. I've already got one duel on my hands."

"Then I won't," Lutyens said.

"So what about it?" Darnell demanded.

"You really fancy the law in the family?"

"I don't, Lucy does."

Blackstone groaned. "Is she serious?"

"Deadly serious," Darnell said.

Blackstone rose unsteadily. "I think it's time I went to bed."

Lutyens stood up, holding the table with one hand. "I think the lush is affecting my brain," he remarked. "I had a few glasses of wine at Longwood. And do you know, as I rode through Jamestown, I could have sworn that I saw Napoleon walking down the road?"

Darnell laughed. Blackstone stared at Lutyens, all the old detective instincts surfacing from the depths of the booze.

Louise Perkins was waiting for Blackstone in his bed. She had applied a little rouge to her cheeks and some lavender water behind her ears and between her breasts; she had dishevelled her hair slightly and she wore only her bodice and stays loosely tied. No man, she thought, certainly no man as virile as Edmund Blackstone, could resist her. She waited impatiently, brooding about her past tactics; indisputably they had been wrong. Blackstone was not the sort of man to appreciate the sophisticated flirt; the fluttering of eyelids to the accompaniment of the harp, the teasing chatter, the rendezvous in the rose garden, the clandestine meeting in the house of a friend, the friend conveniently away. No, she had misjudged her man because she had never met such a man before. She shivered expectantly. Where was he? Damn him!

It was a fine night, the sky glittering with stars, the moon a scimitar. She could picture him now, standing beside the bed, the pale light finding the muscles and scars on his body, polishing his black hair, exaggerating the cruelty on his face, a cruelty which lifted suddenly when he smiled. But it was the cruelty which occupied her thoughts at the moment. She imagined the fierce pressure of his lips, the hardness of his body. I, too, am cruel, she thought; we are of the same stock; but he hadn't yet given her the opportunity to exert her cruelty; that would come when he sought her body for the second time and she denied him and returned to her handsome and boring husband. Or would it? The disturbing thought occurred to her that this would be cruelty to herself, a self-inflicted wound. She fidgeted in the bed. Where was the arrogant bastard?

Faintly, she heard footsteps in the passage. She lit the candle-lantern and waited, elbow on the pillow, resting her head in her hand, the warm slopes of her breasts naked. She tried to control her trembling which was a contradiction of languid seductress. The footsteps grew nearer, stopped.

The handle of the door turned and Lucinda Darnell walked in.

She stood there, hands on her hips. "So," she said, "m'lady has grown tired of waiting, eh? M'lady has shown herself in her true colours at last. M'lady is nothing more than a common judy." She took a step towards the bed. "I don't allow common little judies to dab it up in my establishment," she said, pulling up the sleeves of her dress.

Louise sat upright in the bed. She said: "Get out of here you slut."

"Me get out of here? Me in my own tavern?"

"Your father's tavern. And this isn't your room. Now get out."

Lucinda's eyes glittered in the candlelight. "Maybe the room isn't mine, my dear, but I've warmed that bed a few times. I've always found it very accommodating." She looked around the room. "Time m'lady was taught a lesson," she said, picking up Blackstone's riding crop from a chair.

"You wouldn't dare."

"I've fought better than you in my time. I scratched out the eyes of a revenue officer in the old days." She flexed the small whip. "Out of that bed you common little tail."

"You keep your distance, you trollop. Blackie will be here in a minute and he'll see to you."

"Blackie, is it? Very familiar, aren't we. The French mistress, the nurse, the whore!" Lucinda spat. "I'll give you Blackie, my dear. Now, out of that bed."

"You touch me and I'll have you put under lock and key. The Governor and I are good friends."

"Trying to dab it up with the Lackey, are you? Not much joy there I shouldn't think, he'd be too scared of creasing his uniform. And in any case, by the time I've finished with you your nancy will be so sore you won't be able to walk to your carriage."

From the parlour they heard laughter and the sound of breaking glass.

Louise opened her mouth to scream.

Lucinda leapt forward and grabbed her bodice; the fabric tore, exposing firm white breasts. The sight of them increased Lucinda's fury. She raised the crop and brought it down but Louise wriggled to one side and the pillow took the first blow.

With Lucinda off balance Louise clawed at her face with long pink fingernails. Blood flowed down one cheek.

Lucinda drew back panting. "You bitch. I'll kill you for that."

Louise was out of the bed crouching beside the table. She hoped she looked craven with fear because it would give her an advantage; the only emotion she felt, after the initial shock, was excitement that was almost a lust.

"You might well cower," Lucinda breathed, moving round the room. "You might well grovel, my dear. You'll rue the day you ever tried to bed down with Blackie."

Snake-like, she lashed out with the riding crop, but Louise caught it, leaping to her feet at the same time. Silently they wrestled with the crop. Louise realised she hadn't the other girl's strength, but she didn't try and escape through the door. The thought of inflicting pain, even receiving it, gave her a fierce pleasure.

Lucinda broke away, holding the crop. "Now," she said, "now you're for it, my pretty one." She raised the whip and lashed at Louise's face; Louise ducked and stumbled, falling across the bed. Lucinda fell on her, lifted her skirts and brought the crop down on her bare buttocks.

Louise squealed. Lay still for a moment as a second lash bit into her flesh, then twisted violently to one side so that both of them fell on the floor, Louise on top. With her fists she pummelled Lucinda's face. Lucinda squirmed and kicked, her foot catching the table. The candle-lantern fell to the ground and a flame caught the overhanging sheet.

Louise fell to one side. They broke. They were on their feet, facing each other, the crop lying between them. The flame accelerated and ran across the bed.

Breathing heavily and coughing as the smoke reached their lungs, they both went for the riding crop. Lucinda's dress was torn and they were both bare to the waist. They clawed and gouged and bit and that was how Blackstone found them, half-naked bodies glistening in the glare of the blazing bed-linen.

He grabbed a jug of water and poured it over the fire, then upturned the bed, stamping out the rest of the flames on the floor.

The girls parted, panting.

"For God's sake," Blackstone said, "what is it about this room? Why does it always have to be wrecked?"

"I found your fancy woman in your bed," Lucinda said.

"Your whore attacked me," Louise said.

"Ladies, ladies ..." Blackstone began.

"There are no ladies here," Lucinda interrupted.

Blackstone regarded their nudity. There wasn't much to choose between them, he decided; they were both magnificent women.

They covered their breasts, Louise feeling her rump, Lucinda dabbing at the scratches on her cheek. Blackstone opened the window to let the smoke out. "Where the hell am I going to sleep now?" he asked.

"I can tell you where you're not going to sleep," Lucinda told him. "And that's with me."

"Nor me," Louise Perkins said. "I don't like sharing anything."

The girls glanced at each other, half-smiling. Lucinda suggested they go and bathe their wounds; Louise accepted the offer and Blackstone was left with a broken bed and a mess of charred linen. It rather looked, he thought, as if he was to be deprived of one of the few consolations of life on St Helena.

Next morning at dawn, his instincts re-awakened by Lutyens's remarks, he took a dinghy and rowed round the harbour. His head ached and it was difficult to think logically. Who was the short plumpish man Lutyens had seen walking round Jamestown? Surely not Napoleon; the Scourge of Europe was mortally ill at Longwood and, despite Lowe's cynicism, had less than a month to live according to those who recognised the symptoms of death. The sunken eyes, the grey pallor, the final mask assembling.

Was it the same man he had seen in the cave at the end of the passage leading from the Good Neighbour? I should have explored the harbour before, he thought guiltily. And would have done if my loyalties hadn't been divided; if Lowe hadn't tilted the balance in favour of Bonaparte. Was there even now an underwater vessel lurking on the bed of the ocean waiting to spirit the dying emperor away? Was it possible that freedom would cure the liver malady endemic to this graveyard of an island? If there is a plan afoot, Blackstone wondered, what should I do? He knew his true allegiance lay to the Crown of England, even if it meant thwarting the last spasm of a dying emperor, the greatest soldier the world had known since Caesar.

But could he do it?

Again he evaded the question by reminding himself that it was an impossibility for a man as sick as Napoleon to walk to the end of the garden let alone escape under the British blockade.

The sea was calm, the skyline greenish with milky light beginning to wash the sky. A few incurious gulls floated on the placid water; the merchant ships in the bay moved gently on an imperceptible swell; his oars made snug sounds in the water.

Somewhere here was an exit to the tunnel. Somewhere here was the answer to the questions which had lain dormant in Blackstone's mind since the garrison ball. An academic exercise, maybe, but at least it was helping him regain some of his self-respect.

He counted the ships in the bay. Fourteen, one more than yesterday. Which was the newcomer? There it was – a brig anchored on the far side of the other merchant ships.

Blackstone pulled lazily at the oars. From the stale fumes of last night's liquor another query arose. What memory was it that the references to Dartmouth had stirred? Blackstone shook his head, sending a stab of pain from his forehead to the back of his neck.

He determined to drink less. Although, with Louise Perkins and Lucinda Darnell ganging up against him, there wouldn't be much solace of another variety.

He breathed deeply of the morning air. It smelled clean and fresh; from the town he caught a whiff of bread baking. It made him feel hungry. There was movement on the ships and, high on the cliffs, scarlet-jacketed look-outs were stirring, going about their dawn duties on the most dreaded posting in the British Army.

Blackstone pulled harder at the oars, watching the swirls of water recede. A fish popped, a crab stranded on a rock waved its claws at him; there was a sharp explosion as the dawn cannon was fired. Another dreary day on the island was beginning as life ran out for the fallen leader at Longwood House.

Blackstone was rowing towards Munden's point, one of the two jaws of Jamestown, when he found the entrance to the tunnel blocked by a boulder. He threw down a small anchor and climbed warily ashore, Manton in one hand.

He pushed the boulder but it wouldn't budge. He cast his mind back to his flasherman days. How did they move the "doors" of secret passages on the coast of Devon. There was usually a trick to it, he remembered. Underneath the boulder he spotted a stone the size of a cannon-ball. He leaned with his back against the cliff and pushed it with his heel; the stone shot out and the boulder moved, leaving a space big enough for him to climb through.

He cocked the Manton and climbed through. Water dripped from the walls and red, rodent eyes stared from the darkness.

His eyes grew accustomed to the light. The kegs of contraband liquor were still stacked in cavities in the walls, rum, brandy, Hollands. One hollow was filled with dusty bottles of Graves and Sauterne. Blackstone stuck the Manton in his belt; his head still ached and he decided to cure it with a hair of the dog's nose, tapping a keg of Hollands and half-filling a glass he found on a desk.

The desk faced a small aperture in the wall through which he could see and smell the sea. He sat down facing the entrance to the cave and glanced through a pile of papers lying on the desk. They were all in French; Blackstone wished he had listened more attentively to Louise Perkins. Beside the papers stood a bottle of black ink, a quill, a lorgnette, a bag of liquorice sweets and a gold snuffbox. Had Napoleon sat here writing his memoirs, taking snuff, sucking the black sweets he loved? Blackstone sipped his gin, listening to the gurgle of water; he picked up the gold snuffbox; it still felt warm to his touch. Just the warmth of gold, perhaps, or his imagination. Where are you, my little corporal? Blackstone picked up the quill, feeling that he was close to the soul of greatness.

He examined the papers more closely. One was a letter signed Roubeaud and there were references to Napoleon in it. The name stirred a memory. Thoughtfully Blackstone finished his gin. Who the hell was Roubeaud? He left the papers as he had found them and returned to the dinghy.

Blackstone pulled strongly across the harbour. Then he remembered: Napoleon was supposed to have a double, a rifleman named Roubeaud.

He stopped rowing as the implications presented themselves. Who had he and Lutyens seen: Napoleon or Roubeaud?

And who was the man dying at Longwood House?

CHAPTER THREE

Blackstone said: "I want you to get into his room and take a good look at him."

Lutyens shook his head. "Too late, Blackie, I resigned over this damned book I received on behalf of the 20th. You've never heard of anything quite so petty. The Lackey carried on as if I had taken part in the Gunpowder Plot."

"Damn." Blackstone dismounted and tethered his horse to an almond tree. They had been fencing in the morning and now they were touring the island. "Who's taken your place?"

Lutyens dismounted. "Fellow called Crokat. Captain William Crokat. There's already talk of him being promoted to major and being given £500 for taking the news of Napoleon's death to the King."

"Napoleon's death?"

"He's dying, Blackie, there's no doubt about that."

"I wonder," Blackstone said thoughtfully.

They began to climb the hills near Stone Top Bay.

"What do you mean, you wonder?"

"Are you sure it's Napoleon dying at Longwood House?"

Lutyens stopped beside a clump of prickly pears. "Have you taken leave of your senses?"

"Not yet. Another couple of weeks on St Helena and I may." He told Lutyens about the cave and the papers.

"After all, you thought you saw Napoleon in Jamestown. Perhaps you did. Perhaps it's Rifleman Roubeaud dying at Longwood."

"Nonsense. I've been there for fourteen months and I'm willing to swear it's Napoleon."

"When did you see him last?"

"Just before he took to his bed."

"So you've no idea who the sick man is?"

"Arnott's seen him."

"But had Arnott ever seen Napoleon before?"

"I don't know," Lutyens said.

They started to walk up the hillside. Blackstone said: "The man dying at Longwood quite possibly is Napoleon. It's absurd to think he's not. And yet. ..." He paused. "It is just possible, isn't it? I don't doubt for one moment that the man you were looking at every day was Napoleon Bonaparte. But another man could have been substituted since the patient took to his bed. You weren't allowed to see him, were you?"

"I suppose not. ..."

"So all we know is that there's a man dying at Longwood. A man answering Napoleon's description, a man with the same symptoms of illness as Napoleon."

Lutyens snapped his fingers. "There's your answer, Blackie. The same symptoms. You're not going to tell me that Napoleon's double has fallen ill with identical symptoms as the Emperor? That," said Lutyens smiling, "is asking too much."

They had reached the top of the hill. Ahead of them lay the sea, lazy and molten, and the islands of Hercules and George speckled with gulls. Beyond the islands a frigate on patrol.

Blackstone picked up a stone and threw it out to sea. "I admit it's asking a lot," he said slowly. "But, you see, I have a theory about that as well."

"I thought you would."

"I know of only one way in which you could induce identical symptoms in two men."

"And that is?"

"Administer the same poison," Blackstone said.

The frigate inched across the horizon and rounded the two small islands.

Lutyens said: "That's ridiculous."

Blackstone shrugged. "Perhaps, but it's interesting. Let's suppose that they've been hatching this plan for a long time. Napoleon is made to appear artificially ill – poisoned in other words – so that Lowe and his spies are prepared for his illness and his death. At the same time the same poison is administered to his double, Rifleman Roubeaud, in the cave under the Good Neighbour. Let us assume that Roubeaud hero-worships Napoleon and is prepared to die for him. Both he and Napoleon are systematically poisoned with equal dosages of poison. The substitution is made and there we have another patient at Longwood with unchanged symptoms. Easy, eh?"

Lutyens looked doubtful. "How would the substitution be made? After all, there's a sentry at every bend in the road."

Blackstone picked a sprig of wild rosemary and stuck it in his button-hole. "As far as I can make out the Army – particularly the 20th – is more loyal to Napoleon than it is to Lowe. Quite understandably. And you know as well as I do that a few kegs of grog can work miracles with soldiers. Ask the excellent Lieutenant Fairfax his views about troops drinking on duty."

Lutyens said: "This man Roubeaud would have to be a fanatic to allow himself to be poisoned."

"Thousands of men have died for Napoleon," Blackstone said. "But I take your point. Which brings me to my other theories."

Lutyens sighed.

"Let us suppose that Rifleman Roubeaud was, in fact, dying. No great sacrifice involved then. All they have to do is to administer poison to Napoleon so that he has the same symptoms as Roubeaud, making damn sure that they don't give him too much. Or perhaps Napoleon was suffering from hepatitis and they gave Roubeaud poison to give him the same symptoms. Or perhaps, being doubles, they've both got the same disease and Roubeaud's has been aggravated with poison to give Lowe a corpse. Anyway it's my guess that this was all set up several months ago but something went wrong. Then it became desperate – Roubeaud was dying and, in any case, they had reached a point where they couldn't administer much more poison to Napoleon or they'd have two corpses on their hands. Two dead Napoleons. What would the Lackey think of that?" Blackstone laughed.

Lutyens said admiringly: "You've got an ingenious mind, Blackie, I'll grant you that."

"Not ingenious. It's all perfectly feasible."

"Except for two things."

"Which are?"

"How did they get Roubeaud on to St Helena? And" – Lutyens paused dramatically – "how are they going to get Boney off?"

"Good questions," Blackstone said. He watched another frigate sail into the seascape and push its way across the blue and gold metal of the sea. "You know as well as I do that it's easy enough to get on to St Helena. Any victualling ship will do the job for a fee. The British aren't looking for bodies coming into St Helena. Only a madman would want to be smuggled *into* this graveyard. All they're looking for is one man being smuggled out."

"Well," Lutyens prompted, "how are they going to get Boney out?"

"The question is: has he gone already?"

"Well, has he?"

"I don't think so," Blackstone said. "There was a half-finished letter in the cave." He took Lutyens's arm. "Let's go back. I think there are going to be developments very soon."

They watched the frigate leave the picture, then started on the downward climb. "There are still a lot of questions to be answered."

"You haven't told me how they're going to get him off the island."

"In a minute," Blackstone said. "Let's get back to the poisoning. My guess is arsenic. But they'd have to be terribly careful. I wonder if they experimented on the unfortunate Cipriani? He was poisoned by all accounts. Another sacrificial offering? And I wonder who's actually administering the poison."

"Presuming that any of this is true...."

"Aye, presuming that." Blackstone gripped Lutyens's arm. "But you've got to admit, culley, that it all falls into place. I thought at first that Antommarchi would be giving the poison. Now I'm not so sure. It seems to me that they deliberately imported a doctor who wouldn't know the difference between the measles and a dose of glim."

"Glim?"

Blackstone laughed. "You wouldn't know about that, eh? The pox to you, Captain Lutyens, sir. Anyway, they brought in a doctor who specialised in carving up corpses and wouldn't have the faintest idea of the difference between arsenic poisoning and hepatitis, the disease of St Helena. But he must have given them a nasty turn when he administered a tartaric emetic. Rather hastening the process, I should think."

"But who did Antommarchi give the emetic to – Napoleon or Roubeaud?"

"Napoleon I should think. Perhaps we'll never know." They reached their horses and mounted. Blackstone stayed still in the saddle for a few moments. "But there's only one question that really matters."

"I can guess." Lutyens stroked his horse's neck. "Where do our loyalties lie?"

"You should know where yours lie, you serve your King."

"And you?"

"And me," Blackstone agreed.

"Then there shouldn't be any problem."

"He's a great man," Blackstone said. He touched the horse with his heels; it began to trot in the direction of Jamestown. Lutyens caught up and they made their way together across farmland embroidered with blossom. "The point is that we – I think I've convinced you sufficiently – suspect that an attempt is to be made to free Napoleon Bonaparte. It is surely our duty to prevent it. Or, at the very least, to tell the authorities. What are we to do, Captain Lutyens?"

"I don't know," Lutyens said.

"Aren't you a man-capable of making decisions?"

"Yes and no," Lutyens replied.

They rode on in silence.

"Perhaps," Lutyens said cautiously, "we should tell someone who won't believe us."

"You don't believe it anyway."

"You're a very convincing sort of fellow," Lutyens said. "But in any case you haven't told me how they're going to spirit Boney away."

Blackstone told him.

Lutyens's disbelief was theatrical. Blackstone reined in his horse and took a newspaper cutting from an inside pocket. "Here, read this. I pinched it from the officers' mess."

Lutyens scanned the cutting from *The Times* about underwater ships. "They don't seem to have been too successful," he remarked.

Blackstone shrugged. "In the 1812 war the Americans tried to sink a seventy-four-gun man-o'-war, the *Ramillies,* in Long Island Sound."

"But they didn't succeed?"

"They didn't succeed but they sailed underneath her three times. It was the explosive charge that didn't work, not the underwater ship. If they managed that nine years ago why shouldn't someone be able to sail under the British fleet in the Atlantic today?"

"Well, perhaps we should tell Lowe," Lutyens said reluctantly. "It's so preposterous that he's not likely to believe it." He brightened. "You know, Blackie, tell it so unconvincingly that he'll merely think you've lost your senses."

Blackstone said: "My problem is deeper than that. I think I'd like to *help* Napoleon escape. Which is totally wrong when you think of all the British soldiers who died fighting him. If only the British had allowed him a little dignity. ..." He spurred the horse into a canter.

Lutyens caught up with him. "What are we going to do?"

"Our duty, of course."

"Tell the Lackey and the Nincompoop?"

"That's not our duty," Blackstone said. "They're inefficient. No, we must do our duty as we see fit. We mustn't confide in any buffoons who would hamper us."

"You mean keep it to ourselves?" Lutyens grinned.

"I mean we should investigate. I wouldn't like the Frogs to think they were getting away with it. A question of vanity, culley."

"And supposing we surprise them in the act."

"An intriguing possibility," Blackstone said.

He spurred his horse and together they galloped towards Jamestown.

On 29 April the patient at Longwood vomited eight times and drank large quantities of orange flower water. On 2–3 May the Abbé Vignali administered extreme unction, anointing eyelids, nostrils, mouth, hands and feet, reciting:

"Deliver, Lord, the soul of your servant, as you delivered Moses from the hands of Pharaoh, King of the Egyptians; deliver, Lord, the soul of your servant, as you delivered St Peter and St Paul from prison."

Later that day the patient was given a massive dose of calomel, a total of ten grains. He lost consciousness and had difficulty in breathing.

On 4 May, while the patient lay in bed, hands crossed over his chest, a cigar-shaped craft was gently lowered from the brig anchored at the outer extremity of the harbour. It had been a day of rain and wind – the wind had uprooted a willow tree at Longwood – and the sea was still choppy. The crew would have preferred a perfectly calm sea but now they had no choice: they had, at the most, twenty-four hours in which to complete their mission.

CHAPTER FOUR

Blackstone laid his guns out on the bed. Two Mantons, duelling pistols, spring-bayonet musket and the new Elisha Collier he had bought in London just before leaving. He examined the Collier: it was an interesting gun because you had to wind it up before firing it. It was one of the new revolvers, single-barrelled with a rotating cylinder carrying bullets and explosive.

Blackstone thought the Collier was an interesting experiment and totally unreliable.

He picked up the duelling pistols with their hooked butts covered with cross-hatching, the whole stock finely balanced to help the duellist raise his arm and fire without sighting. Here, in the stock, was the gunmaker's craft, and in the triggers with their feather pressures so that the barrel didn't waver when you pulled it. Blackstone took out the powder flask, bullet mould and cleaning rods from their green baize nests and cleaned them. He oiled the guns and polished them with love.

He had turned his attention to the French stiletto when Englebert Lutyens burst into the room, his amiable face looking as excited as it was possible for it to look.

Blackstone said: "I should try knocking next time. You nearly got this through your throat." He balanced the knife on his hand.

Lutyens sat down. "You wait till you hear what I've got to tell you."

"I'm waiting," Blackstone said.

There was a knock on the door and a girl came in with a plate of hot buttered toast, a cup and saucer and an elegant silver teapot. Blackstone looked at the teapot with interest: it bore a close resemblance to some plate reported stolen from the Travellers' Club in Pall Mall. "And another cup," he said to the girl.

"You lead a hard life," Lutyens remarked, waiting for Blackstone to ask him about his news.

"I'd rather be chasing a footpad up Ludgate Hill in a blizzard than sitting here eating hot buttered toast."

"You won't be sitting here much longer."

"All right," Blackstone said, "Out with it."

"It looks as if it's on for tonight."

"What, the escape?"

Lutyens nodded, checks flushed in his languid face. The girl came in with another cup and saucer and Blackstone poured the tea.

"Tell me about it," Blackstone said.

Sipping his tea, Lutyens told him that word had spread throughout the island about his quarrel over the book he had accepted from Napoleon. The story, of course, had taken wings and, according to the gossips, there had been a stand-up row between the Governor and Lutyens, culminating with Lutyens stating that his allegiance was with Emperor Bonaparte. Emperor, not General as Lowe had decreed. There was speculation that Lutyens would be court-martialled and might even face a charge of treason.

"Anyway," Lutyens told Blackstone, "the point is that people are firmly convinced that I'm on Boney's side."

"So is most of the island on his side. So is half Britain, come to that."

"Wait." Lutyens put down his cup and held up his hand. "Wait, Blackie, my boy. The point is that someone approached me to help them, thinking that I would do anything to spite Lowe. They wanted me to help them create a diversion on the other side of the island and spike the warning cannon at Alarm House."

Blackstone looked interested. "Who approached you?" He put down his cup of tea and stared at Lutyens.

"You'll never guess."

Blackstone said irritably: "We're not playing guessing games. Who was it?"

"Captain Randolph Perkins," said Lutyens.

"It falls into place now," Blackstone said a little later. "He was one of the couriers, I suppose, bringing the latest information about the underwater vessel." He paced the room while Lutyens, exhausted by all his talk, lounged in the easy chair. "It never occurred to me that the British would be involved in this. I must be losing my touch. I suppose they brought the vessel on a British ship so that no one would challenge it."

Lutyens said: "I shouldn't think there's any question of Perkins acting because of the feeling in Britain. Swag is all he's interested in. Promised me £250 as a matter of fact."

Blackstone raised his eyebrows. "He must be getting a fair bit of blunt then."

"There's a lot of money involved, Blackie. Boney might seem poor on St Helena but he's got loot hidden away all over the world. Brother Joseph must be good for a few thousand and I'll wager he's putting up the funds. Marie-Louise will have to watch out," he said thoughtfully, "if Boney gets away and finds her dabbing it up with someone else."

"And what about Louise Perkins? Is she up to her crooked eyes in it?"

Lutyens said: "Apparently so. Napoleon took quite a fancy to you. Thought you would be the one to help him in the British camp. Not such a bad guess, eh, Blackie?" Lutyens stretched. "So he told Louise to get you into bed and persuade you to help. But she failed apparently." He looked slyly at Blackstone. "I find that hard to believe, Blackie."

"On my mother's grave," Blackstone said. "Of course it also explains why they had to call off the duel. Perkins would have been sent home in disgrace and that would have been the end of their little scheme – and the money." He laughed. "Well, well, poor old Louise. And she got her nancy trimmed into the bargain." He took out his Breguet. "What time is it going to happen?"

"In the early hours of the morning," Lutyens said. "That's all I know. I've got to meet Perkins in half an hour and tell him if I'm ready to help."

"Good." Blackstone tucked a pistol into his belt. "Keep the appointment and meet me back here at seven. I've got things to do."

Lutyens stood up. "Tell me, Blackie, do you really think the man at Longwood is Roubeaud?"

"That," Blackstone said, "is what we've got to find out."

"And can we betray Lowe? Betray the King?"

"Betray? That's a strong word." Blackstone stared in the tin mirror to see if he detected treachery in his features. "I don't know. Let's find out what's happening first."

He picked up the Collier, then put it back in its case. Tonight, he thought, he might need a weapon more reliable than a gun that you had to wind up.

At Longwood House the patient developed hiccups, then fell into a delirium, calling out: "What is the name of my son?" When he was calmer they applied a sponge dampened with sugared water to his lips.

The air in the underwater ship was putrid, the light from the candle-lantern as uncertain as a will-o'-the-wisp. The Cornish captain with the bullet-scarred face wound the handle attached to the screw, four of the crew worked the oars – the dead man had been replaced – while the fifth stood on the steps peering through the observation porthole.

A little water leaked through the leather oar-locks. Sweat slid down the men's bodies. Fear was cold inside them. The sea all around was like black treacle.

One of the oarsmen said: "Can't you see anything?" His voice was flaky with fear.

"Not a bloody thing," the observer said.

"We should never have done it," the oarsman said. "How do we know we'll ever get up again."

The captain said coldly: "We did last time. Why not now?"

"It was daylight then."

Another oarsman said: "We should have waited till it got calmer."

"They said it had to be tonight."

"*They*! They don't have to go under the water." He stopped rowing. "Let's get back to the surface, for God's sake."

The captain touched the barrel of the pistol beside him. "Keep rowing you swab. If we surface now we'll come up under a British frigate."

"We might be heading out into the middle of the Atlantic for all you know."

"Why should we? We haven't turned. You're all pulling with the same strength."

"How do we know when to surface? I mean, how do you know we're not going to smash straight into the rocks?"

"It's all been calculated," the captain said. "Everything's been carefully calculated. Like us being English. Who would have thought the English would try to rescue Boney?"

The first oarsman said: "Was it all calculated when they lost the first ship?" He shivered despite the sweat.

"That was a mistake."

"I'll say it was, culley."

Something phosphorescent glided past one of the portholes. When it had gone the darkness seemed thicker than before. The air smelled of rotting vegetation despite the fan which the observer was now operating. The captain said: "We'd best stop talking, it's as if we're swallowing the air."

The *Shark*'s dark body glided on, ten feet below the surface, her airpipe just cutting it.

Number Thirteen said: "It looks to me as if this will be the last time. They say Napoleon's almost dead."

Hannibal shrugged his huge shoulders in the darkness. "This one should buy me a ticket to England."

They stopped in the shadow of a warehouse on the quayside. "This one should be easy." The little Chinaman's voice fluttered like wind-chimes. "Are the bottles all there?"

"They're all here," Hannibal said, pointing at six tea-chests almost hidden beside the wall of the warehouse. "But I think it's risky, right in the middle of the harbour."

Number Thirteen's reedy voice was full of confidence. "The look-outs have been given brandy and it is the British Navy that wants the wine. In any case, everyone's concentrating on what's happening at Longwood House."

"I hope you're right." Hannibal pointed across the water.

"What's that?"

Number Thirteen stared hard. "I can't see anything." Some of the confidence had left his voice. "Not another monster, Hannibal?" He tried to laugh but the notes in the wind-chimes had cracked.

Gun in hand, Blackstone made his way along a corridor in the Good Neighbour to Jack Darnell's room.

Lutyens had met Perkins and told him he couldn't go through with it. "After all, you can't really blame me, Blackie, can you? It would be the end of my career and, in any case, I was never an adventurer. Not a cavalier if you know what I mean."

Blackstone told Lutyens he knew what he meant.

According to Lutyens, a diversion was to be made near the islands of Egg and Bird, where Lieutenant Fairfax had made his bid for historical recognition. A barrel of gunpowder was to be exploded; but the actual escape attempt would be in Jamestown harbour, such an obvious place that – the French believed – security was less strict. The attempt had to be tonight, Lutyens had explained, because when the patient at Longwood died, an autopsy might reveal the body wasn't Napoleon's. At any rate, that's what the French were saying.

"I don't know so much about the French," Blackstone had replied. "As far as I can make out this is a British plot."

Which was why he was making his way warily towards Darnell's bedroom.

He didn't knock. Just as blind people developed other senses so one-armed men were surprisingly nimble with the good arm. Gently, he tried the handle. It moved easily and Blackstone kicked the door open.

Darnell was sitting at a table with his wooden arm in front of him. "Hallo, Blackie," he said, "I've been half expecting you for some time."

Blackstone went in, the barrel of the Manton aimed at Darnell's head.

Darnell said: "Don't blow the other arm off, Blackie, I'm not very good at milling with two feet."

"The pistol," Blackstone said, pointing at the brass-barrelled Nock on the table beside Darnell's wooden arm. "Knock it on the floor and don't, for God's sake Jack, try and use it."

Darnell pushed the pistol on to the floor. They both gazed at it for a moment.

Darnell said: "You're very cautious, Blackie, in your dealings with a one-armed man."

"I know you of old, Jack. I think you're twice as dangerous since you lost your arm."

Darnell grinned; it reminded Blackstone of a chasm suddenly opening on a rocky hillside. "What do you want, Blackie, as if I didn't know."

Blackstone prowled round the room.

Darnell picked up his arm. "Perhaps you could help me with this, Blackie. Lucy usually straps it on for me. The old stump's been paining me of late."

"What about your conscience, Jack? I should think that's been troubling you a mite."

Darnell handed him the wooden arm with the hook in it. "Be a good chap, Blackie ...."

"No tricks, mind."

"No tricks," Darnell promised.

Blackstone strapped the limb on warily, reflecting that Darnell's promises were as substantial as counterfeit money. Where, he asked Darnell, was Napoleon Bonaparte.

Darnell began expertly to fill his clay pipe with one hand. "The question is, Blackie, how much do you know? Quite a bit, I'll wager, or else you wouldn't be here. But then again, you might know very little. Trapping an old sea-dog into making a confession, eh?"

Blackstone said: "I know you've been helping the French to get Napoleon off St Helena."

Darnell sucked at his pipe for a while before replying: "I don't even know if that's true, my covey. And that's God's truth."

"Pull the other leg," Blackstone said, "it's got bells on it."

"It's as true as the day I was born." Darnell blew a jet of grey smoke across the table at Blackstone. "Tell me what you know, Blackie, and then I might be able to help you."

Blackstone shrugged. "As you wish. I think you and Lucy came over here to organise the escape. An expert smuggler such as yourself, Jack, what better man to do the job? You know the sea, its tides and its mood, as well as I know the inside of a tankard of ale."

Darnell held up his wooden arm. "One moment, Blackie. I'm not admitting nothing." He paused. "Not denying it neither. I might be the cove you describe, then again I might not. But you've got one thing wrong – Lucy didn't know anything about anything."

Blackstone stared hard at Darnell. "Are you telling the truth, Jack?"

"Why should I lie?"

Blackstone believed him; perhaps, he thought, because I want to.

"Let's hear the rest of it, Blackie."

"So you found yourself a nice little tavern in Jamestown and rigged it up like the old Mount Pleasant. I shouldn't imagine they gave you all the blunt at once. I wouldn't in their place. I would say it was brought out by various couriers such as Captain Randolph Perkins." Blackstone watched Darnell's face for a reaction; but it was difficult to identify expressions on the craggy landscape with its thicket of beard. "I'd watch Captain Perkins if I were you, Jack. Has he made the final payment yet?"

Darnell blew a smoke ring from the corner of his mouth. "That's a leading question, Blackie. Like, Have I stopped beating my wife yet?"

"The last payment is the big one, isn't it, Jack?"

Darnell didn't reply.

"I wouldn't trust a man with all those sparklers on his hands. No more would I trust a man who lets his wife be used for his own ends. Have you seen him today, Jack?"

Blackstone stood up and strode round the room thinking. If he had concentrated as hard as this in the first place he would have solved the whole thing. He took some snuff and went on:

"Perkins thought I was dangerous. So he employed a Negro to kill me – and use a Chinese knife to confuse matters – before I could do any damage. A blackbird," Blackstone said, sitting in front of Darnell, "who couldn't sing. But even dumb blackbirds can make themselves understood and when I recognised him at Plantation House he had to be disposed of. This is what I think happened that night."

"So now you only *think*?"

"Watch your step, Jack. I also think you doctored my rum that first night to make things easy for the Negro, but I'll overlook it for the moment." He paused. "Now, I think the blackbird let it be known that I'd spotted him at Plantation House. God knows, this place has got as many spies as rats on it. So Perkins told him to get away from Plantation House, get into my room and finish the job."

Another smoke ring eddied from Darnell's lips.

"But Perkins knew I wouldn't be caught so easily twice. So he sent a messenger to the Good Neighbour. The message was: Kill the Negro. God knows, Jack, some of your customers would slit their mothers' throats for a couple of sovereigns."

"I don't know anything about that," Darnell said firmly.

"It doesn't matter. Anyway, someone was employed to silence a dumb blackbird who could, perhaps, talk with his claws."

"You spin a pretty yarn," Darnell said. "I'll grant you that. What about a grog to oil your throat?"

"I'll get it." Blackstone took a bottle of brandy from the top of a chest of drawers and poured them both a nip. He went on: "What puzzles me is why I wasn't killed when I found the tunnel."

He waited until Darnell said: "You don't expect me to answer that do you, Blackie?"

"Answer me this: Did Lucy know about the contraband liquor?"

Darnell looked at him warily. "She might have."

"Then this is what I think happened." What I hope happened, he thought. "Lucy came into the parlour and realised I'd found the tunnel. She came down just as you, or whoever it was, knocked me out. You couldn't finish me off then, could you, Jack? By the way, what did you hit me with? That?" Blackstone asked, pointing at the wooden arm.

"I wouldn't want to break it on your skull," Darnell said. He tossed back his brandy in one neat movement.

"Anyway, when you heard Lucy coming you got your *guest* out of the way. Who was it at that time? – Napoleon or Roubeaud?" Blackstone leaned across the table. "I'd dearly like to know that, Jack."

"You're the yarn-spinner, Blackie, you tell me."

Blackstone shrugged. "Anyway, Napoleon, in his wisdom, had decided that I might be of more use than harm so they decided to let me live. Decent of them," he said reflectively.

"Is that the end of the tale?"

Blackstone shook his head. "Not quite."

"Are you going to try and explain how anyone can get Napoleon through the blockade?"

"I'm afraid I am, Jack. And you're not going to like it."

Darnell knocked out his pipe.

Blackstone said: "We were talking about Dartmouth the other night. It stirred some memory and I couldn't for the life of me remember what it was. I remembered today. When we last had a grog together in the Castle there was talk of a monster in the River Dart."

Darnell capitulated. "You seem to know most of it, Blackie. They built the underwater ship up the Dart and held the first trials opposite the Castle."

Blackstone grinned. "Near a rock called Blackstone if I'm not mistaken."

"Aye," Darnell agreed, "there's a rock called that all right. A big dark rough bastard like its namesake."

"So what went wrong with the plan?"

"A young blade by the name of Fairfax fired his cannon and the underwater ship went under the water and never came up again."

"So they had to get another one out from England?"

"That they did," Darnell said.

"And it's here now?"

"I couldn't say for sure."

"Oh yes you could," Blackstone said mildly. "What's more it's all laid on for tonight in the early hours and you're going to take me down to your cave."

"Am I?" Darnell stared at Blackstone, his eyes cold. "Am I, culley?"

Blackstone picked up the Manton. "It's up to you, Jack Darnell. I can't imagine you pulling much ale without any arms."

"Do what you please. I'm not taking you nowhere. I'm not a nose, Blackie, and you've no right to ask me to peach on anyone. Besides," Darnell said, "I'm not so sure you want to stop him leaving. These walls are thin, Blackie, and I've heard you talking."

"I don't know what I want. But I'll tell you what I don't want – I don't want to be beaten by Perkins."

Darnell poured more brandy. After a while he said: "Maybe you won't be hoodwinked by anyone."

"And what's that supposed to mean?"

Darnell paused before speaking. "I'm not so sure that it's Boney they're going to take away. I think they may have left it too late. Maybe he's so ill they can't move him."

"Then why the hell are they bothering to go through with the plan?"

"Let's say the Frogs are fond of having the last word. Let's say Boney dies tomorrow up at Longwood House and is buried with all the usual pomp and ceremony. Lowe would look pretty stupid, wouldn't he, if Napoleon – or someone very much like him – turned up in America?"

Blackstone drank some brandy and rolled it meditatively round his mouth. Who was the man waiting in the cave below? Emperor or rifleman? There was only one way to find out. He waved the Manton at Darnell. "You lead the way," he said.

Darnell shook his head determinedly. "You can blow my brains out if you like, Blackie, but I'm not taking you."

"I can wait," Blackstone said, settling himself in the chair. "The word is that the attempt won't be made until the early hours."

Darnell glared at him.

Blackstone said: "But don't forget, culley, that Perkins has your blunt and I wouldn't trust him farther than the parlour of the Good Neighbour with it."

A breeze hustled the clouds swiftly across the sea; reinforcements took their place but, now and again, the harbour was lit with moonlight making a frozen tableau out of it. The top of a pipe which had been moving slowly towards the shore stopped, its wake swirling for a few moments. Beneath the silvered surface of the water there was turbulence and new waves glowing with phosphorescence glided towards the cliffs of Munden's Point. Outside the harbour a British Naval frigate sailed past. The time was 12.58 a.m. on 5 May.

Beside the warehouse Hannibal and Number Thirteen strained their eyes. The Chinaman said: "You must have been seeing things." You big, superstitious idiot, he implied.

"I saw it," Hannibal said obstinately.

"What, the monster?" Number Thirteen laughed nervously to display oriental superiority.

"I saw something."

"A porpoise, probably."

"It wasn't a porpoise last time. Look." Hannibal pointed out to sea again, almost knocking Number Thirteen over with his hand. In the brief moonlight a shape was making its way towards them.

Number Thirteen laughed happily. "It's the cutter. In ten minutes we'll be able to hand over the wine for the last time. How about that, eh? For the very last time."

Hannibal moaned softly and grabbed the Chinaman's arm, almost breaking the frail bones.

In the path of the cutter a shape was rising laboriously from the deep. There was a light shining dimly inside its great head and water was streaming from its flanks.

Then clouds covered the moon again.

CHAPTER FIVE

There was a second passage leading from behind the bar in the parlour down to the cave. Darnell went first with Blackstone behind him, prodding him with the barrel of his pistol. It was 1 a.m.

"No tricks, mind," Blackstone whispered.

"I'm only taking you in case that bastard Perkins is trying to get away with the swag."

"Then you'd best hurry up."

The door to the passage was a huge empty barrel which smelled of wine that has turned to vinegar. They climbed through the barrel and down a winding flight of stone steps. Darnell carried a lantern and once again Blackstone could see red eyes in front of him, hear the scurry of rodent feet.

After a. hundred yards or so the tunnel joined another; the one he had passed along before, Blackstone presumed. He jammed the pistol into Darnell's back. "Easy now, culley. You go ahead as we planned. I'll be a little way behind you – but you're a fine big target for a bullet."

Darnell swore softly.

They could see the glow from the cave now, hear the lapping of water and the sound of voices.

"Early, aren't they?" Blackstone whispered.

151

Darnell whispered back: "Perkins said two o'clock, the bastard."

"Sounds like you've been double-crossed, Jack Darnell."

Darnell quickened his pace, slipping on the wet stones. He rounded the corner. Blackstone followed. The only person in the cave was Randolph Perkins, standing at the gap leading to the sea.

Beyond him Blackstone caught a glimpse of a figure standing in the moonlight. A short, plump figure. Then the moonlight was gone and with it the silhouette.

Blackstone ran towards the opening as Perkins fired his pistol. The ball caught Blackstone in the arm, throwing him back on to the ground. He shouted to Darnell: "Get him, Jack. He's making off with your swag."

Blackstone fired the Manton from the ground but the ball smashed into the roof of the cave. The noise hurt his eardrums; blood ran warmly down his arm.

Darnell ran straight at Perkins. Perkins's second bullet smashed his wooden arm and the smell of scorched wood joined the reek of exploded gunpowder. The hook clattered on the ground beside Blackstone. He grabbed it, stood up and lurched towards Perkins.

Perkins turned in the entrance, a smoking pistol in each hand. He threw one at Blackstone. It hit Blackstone on the forehead but still he went at Perkins. In a futile gesture Perkins pulled the trigger of the second pistol, then dropped it.

He shouted: "There's a lot of money in it, Blackie. Come with …"

Blackstone hit him with the curve of the hook, trying not to rip his face with the point. His wounded arm was full of pain and he felt a cold sickness rising through his body.

The force of the blow pushed Perkins through the gap between the boulder and the cliff-face. Blackstone went after him, trying to cover-up as Perkins's knee came at him.

Then they were struggling on the narrow ledge above the rocks. Blackstone was vaguely aware of shouting and shots in the harbour. He brought his instep down Perkins's shin and heard a bone break in Perkins's foot. Perkins stepped back, into the entrance, kicking the stone that controlled the boulder with his uninjured foot.

The stone did its job and the boulder closed on Perkins, crushing him; only the diamonds on his fingers remained intact.

The dinghy had reached the *Shark* and, once again, Blackstone made out the now familiar silhouette of the short, fat man. There were other figures on the streaming deck firing at the naval cutter that had almost cut them in half. The sailors on the cutter were firing back, shouting and arguing in confusion.

The hatch opened and the portly figure disappeared.

Blackstone heard a sailor shout: "I've been hit."

"But who's firing at us?" another asked.

The firing wavered for a moment. One by one the figures on the *Shark* were disappearing. Finally only one was left, the skipper. He took a last shot at the cutter and vanished.

The *Shark* began to submerge.

"Christ," said a sailor, "she's sinking." He aimed a pistol at the *Shark* and Blackstone saw a burst of fire in the tower.

Would it suffer the same fate as the submarine Lieutenant Fairfax had disturbed? At that moment Blackstone didn't care. With blood streaming down his arm he kicked the efficient stone and squeezed past the remains of Captain Randolph Perkins, late of the 45th Foot, Grenadier Company.

"You see I was right," moaned Hannibal, who had been paralysed by fear. "It was a monster and it was breathing smoke and flames."

He looked round but he was alone. Once again the imperturbable Chinaman had fled.

On the ground Hannibal noticed the Chinaman's purse. He picked it up thoughtfully. Perhaps he would be able to sail to England first class.

At 3.43 a.m. the patient at Longwood House murmured incoherently: "France – armée – tête d'armée – Josephine."

Shortly afterwards he fell to the floor, struggling with Montholon.

At dawn on the 5th he was calm but his breathing was faint. He was still like that at 5.41 in the afternoon when the sun set and the usual cannon was fired.

He sighed twice – at 5.47 and 5.48.

At 5.49 he stopped breathing.

At 5.51 Antommarchi closed his eyelids and pronounced the patient dead.

Lucinda Darnell brought the news to Blackstone, sitting up in bed, his arm in a sling.

"The Neighbour's dead," she told him.

"A man died," Blackstone said, "but who was he?" He looked closely at Lucinda to see if she reacted.

But she said: "Whatever do you mean, Blackie?" And Blackstone saw only innocence in her eyes. Innocence and a look of determination that made him vow to catch the next ship back to England.

As she slipped off her dress and climbed into bed beside him, he was still wondering: Who died? Who – if anyone – managed to escape?

HISTORICAL NOTE

A certain Captain Thomas Johnson, ex-British Naval Officer and smuggler, was offered £40,000 by the French to construct an underwater ship that could take Napoleon away from St Helena. Captain Johnson had assisted the American Robert Fulton with his experiments; he had also run contraband to America. If the plan was successful he was promised yet another £40,000 – a fortune "beyond the dreams of avarice" as it was described. But, or so it is said, the plan was forestalled by the death of Napoleon.

There has always been a good deal of speculation about the possibility that Napoleon escaped from St Helena. One school asserts that he escaped to rule over a kingdom of Negroes; another that he died selling spectacles in Verona; yet another that he was observed tending his garden in Philadelphia. Another persistent theory is that a rifleman named Roubeaud, Napoleon's double, was substituted for the ex-Emperor.

Anything is possible – particularly in a work of fiction!

Certainly mystery has always surrounded the cause of death of the patient at Longwood. The official post-mortem recorded a cancerous ulcer of the stomach. But this was a convenient diagnosis for Lowe because it was the same disease that killed Napoleon's father. Antommarchi and a Dr Short both observed abnormality of the liver, but Lowe would not allow this to be recorded, presumably because he had always accused Napoleon of malingering. Even today there is still dispute about the cause of death – hepatitis and a peptic ulcer and Fröhlich's Disease have all been considered. Cancer of the liver, however, appears to be the most common theory, with the inevitable rider that, in reality, Napoleon died of boredom, frustration and despair.

One other medical discovery is pertinent. A tuft of hair allegedly taken from Napoleon's scalp was recently examined and found to contain an abnormally high arsenic content. It has been suggested, therefore, that the Emperor was poisoned; the counter argument is that arsenic was used freely in medication at the beginning of the nineteenth century and the body built up a high tolerance to it.

There have also been disputes about the authenticity of Napoleon's death mask. It is said that the mask has a low, receding forehead and a weak chin, hardly physical characteristics of a military genius. Again, there are counter arguments. There is also some confusion about how the various masks were taken. Dr Francis Burton, surgeon to the 66th Regiment, for instance, made a plaster cast, but this was taken away from him by Bertrand. Why? Because it would have proved that the dead man wasn't Napoleon? It is a novelist's privilege to speculate beyond the licence of the historian.

Sir Hudson Lowe's part in the closing chapters of Napoleon's life has not been charitably recorded by historians. It is not difficult to see why; to the very end, and beyond, he was petulant and pedantic. Napoleon was buried with full military honours in Geranium Valley, St Helena (his body was much later exhumed and laid to rest on the banks of the Seine). Montholon asked for the following inscription:

Napoléon
Né à Ajaccio le 15 août 1769
Mort à Ste-Hélène le 5 mai 1821

Lowe rejected the suggestion, insisting that the inscription should read Napoleon Bonaparte. The tomb was left without a name.

Readers may be surprised that submarines were operating at this time. In fact, as early as the sixteenth century an Englishman named William Bourne, a gunner under Admiral Sir William Monson, had demonstrated how a craft made with a wooden frame covered with leather could be submerged and rowed beneath the surface; water was used as ballast and the volume of the vessel was changed by contracting the sides with hand vises.

Bourne's research was followed up by a Dutchman, Cornelius van Drebbel. Drebbel designed an underwater ship with a leather bulkhead; when the bulkhead was withdrawn, water poured in through holes in the ship's sides until the upper deck was covered; then, with oars paddling, the vessel sailed along partially submerged. When the leather bulkhead was screwed back, the ship became totally buoyant again – they hoped. According to legend, James I travelled from Westminster to Greenwich in one of Drebbel's wood-and-greased-leather ships. Drebbel also installed air-pipes with a purifying system worked by bellows.

After Drebbel there came a series of designs and, by 1727, fourteen had been patented in England. But the most ambitious and warlike was designed by two French priests, Fathers Mersenne and Fournier, of the Order of Minimes, who devised a vessel with wheels to run along the sea-bed, air-pumps, phosphorescent lighting, big guns and an escape hatch. After that came experiments with leather bottles filled with water ballast which could be expelled by hand.

In 1773 a carpenter named Day experimented with stone ballast, the stones being attached to the outside of the hull and released from inside. Day dived successfully in Plymouth Sound before moving to deeper water. With extra ballast he sank into twenty-two fathoms and never reappeared.

The first known use of an underwater vessel as a weapon came in the second half of the eighteenth century. It was a one-man craft named *Turtle*, invented by David Bushnell of Yale. It was shaped like a pearl and hand-operated by a screw propeller. In 1776 it was manned by Army Sergeant Ezra Lee of Lyme, Connecticut, who tried to attach a charge with a time fuse on the bottom of the British man-o'-war *Eagle*. But the copper bottom was too tough for the screws on the attaching device.

Then came Fulton's "submarine". Napoleon abandoned it – and resurrected it? – because it was too slow. America turned it down and so did Britain – even after it had proved its worth by blowing up a 200-ton brig with 170 lbs of gunpowder. The French Minister of Marine adopted the attitude that attack from underwater was unchivalrous!

What, one wonders, would the good minister have thought of today's weapons?

21192032R00099

Printed in Great Britain
by Amazon